How the Lord Married His Lady

How the Lord Married His Lady

Laura A. Barnes

Laura A. Barnes

2022

First Printing: 2022

ISBN: 9798414503842

Laura A. Barnes

Website: www.lauraabarnes.com

Cover Art by Cheeky Covers

Editor: Telltail Editing

Dedication:

I dedicate this book and the Matchmaking Madness series to all the aunts & uncles who love their nieces & nephews as if they were their own children. You are the essence of a loving bond that strengthens a family. To my Aunt Net: Your encouragement and unconditional love is very much cherished. Thank you very much for the essence you have brought to my life. I love you.

Cast of Characters

Hero ~ Lucas Gray

Heroine ~ Abigail Cason

Uncle Theo ~ Duke of Colebourne

Susanna Forrester ~ Colebourne's sister-in-law

Ramsay Forrester ~ Lady Forrester's husband

Charlotte Holbrooke ~ Colebourne's niece

Jasper Sinclair ~ Charlotte's husband

Evelyn Holbrooke ~ Colebourne's niece

Reese Worthington ~ Evelyn's husband

Gemma Holbrooke ~ Colebourne's niece

Barrett Ralston ~ Gemma's husband

Jacqueline Holbrooke ~ Colebourne's niece

Griffen Kincaid ~ Jacqueline's husband

Duncan Forrester ~ Lady Forrester's son/Colebourne's nephew

Selina Forrester ~ Duncan's wife

Prologue

"Excellent. You are alone. We can have some privacy." Lucas Gray closed the door behind him.

"Yes. I am avoiding Gemma because I grow weary of the same argument," Abigail Cason confided to her dear friend. "Now, Jaqueline has joined the ranks to pressure me into attending the Mitchel's musical this evening. I understand it is a small affair and I would be more than welcome since Lady Mitchel is a dear friend to Aunt Susanna. But I do enjoy the quiet evenings to myself."

Lucas paused at Abigail's comment. He never thought that while they were enjoying themselves, how alone Abigail might be. His family had abandoned her when, their entire lives, they had made sure she was part of them. Then, at the first opportunity, they discarded her. Did Abigail view their enjoyment of London in the same way? Perhaps he was wrong in denying her a chance at a season. No. He must stay firm with his opinion.

Only now, he would remain at home occasionally to keep her company. After appearing briefly at the functions they had accepted invitations to, he would pretend to slip away to carouse with his friends. Instead, he would return home to Abigail. They could play chess, read aloud, or enjoy each other's company with the lively conversations they used to have. He had missed their time spent alone ever since his father threw his mad house party. Since Lucas's arrival in London, his own social activities had filled his time.

No more. Abigail needed to be his first priority now more than ever. Once Gemma and Jacqueline married, Abigail threatened to seek employment. She must understand how important she was to their family. Lucas meant to keep her nearby.

"I am glad you see reason, and I support your decision to stay home. I do not understand this family's madness for you to take part in the season." Lucas unbuttoned his suit coat before sitting in a chair.

"Do you think it is madness?" Abigail asked quietly.

"Of course."

"Why would you say that?"

Lucas swept his hand through the air. "It is more than obvious. You are wise enough to understand how the ton wouldn't accept your presence."

"Perhaps I do not. Please, kind sir, enlighten me."

Lucas tensed at Abigail's tone. The air stilled as it had at breakfast when he tried to make his cousins see reason for why Abigail shouldn't join them for the season. He regarded his friend but couldn't determine her mood. While he caught the underline sarcasm, she appeared serene, which only left him confused about how to proceed. However, she needed to hear the truth, regardless of how it hurt her feelings. He would rather be the villain than allow anyone else the pleasure they would receive by insulting her. Even his own betrothed had tried to tear Abigail apart.

Lucas now held his hands out in a peaceful gesture. "Abigail, you must understand how you hold no standing for my father to present you to society."

Abigail sat up straighter. "I am your uncle's ward."

"You are a servant's daughter."

"Is that how you perceive me?" She pinched her lips.

"I am only trying to show you how others will respond to you at the functions our family will attend."

"How will they respond?" Abigail whispered.

"Who?" Lucas shifted in his chair, uncomfortable with the quietness of Abigail's voice when she asked her questions, ones he tried to avoid answering. But he must if they would help her understand her standing in society.

Abigail sighed. "Let us start with the women. How will they slander me? I am only curious because the ladies I have met have shown me kindness and acceptance."

"Only because my father vetted those ladies before he introduced you to them. If you attend the events, he no longer has control over who you will encounter. If you imagine Lady Selina brutal, she holds nothing on the barracudas who will attack you. Their only purpose is to draw blood."

She looked at him in confusion. "Why would anyone feel the need to attack me?"

"Because they fear you will steal away the gentlemen they have set their eyes upon. The married ones are an entirely different lot."

Abigail looked down at her hands. "How am I a threat to them?"

"They fear their husbands will stray."

Abigail lifted her head. "I still do not understand your point."

Lucas gripped the chair, his knuckles straining. "When you walk into a ballroom, you will become a threat to every female in attendance, even if they seem friendly. The single ladies will fear every gentlemen's attention will focus on you, and the married ladies will fear their husbands will lose interest in them to pursue you. I fear the same. If you were to enter the season, every penniless whoreson gold digger will seek to woo you. Every married gentleman will attempt to lead you astray into a torrid affair.

You are a target, with your innocence only enticing them closer to ruination. I will not allow for a scandal to tarnish your reputation."

Abigail listened to Lucas's passionate speech. Nothing he spoke of shocked her. She understood how the gentlemen would treat her because of her rank in society. Also, the dowry Colebourne gifted her with would release the reprobates in search of coin. In truth, those were the reasons she had avoided attending any social gathering.

Yet she longed to see the elegance Gemma described. Perhaps even to find a kind gentleman to dance with. Hopefully, even form a friendship that would entice the gentleman to offer for her hand in marriage. She had watched Charlotte and Evelyn find love, and Abigail wanted to share the same connection with someone. Maybe over time she would grow to love her husband. Also, Colebourne would never allow Abigail to marry anyone unworthy of her love.

For Lucas to speak of married gentlemen pursuing her into scandalous affairs and her becoming their mistresses only indicated how lowly he regarded her. If he thought these gentlemen could tempt her into a scandalous relationship, then he was under the impression that Abigail held loose morals. Was this because her mother had been an unmarried servant with a child? Abigail was unclear of her mother's predicament, but she knew in her heart that her mother's reasons were valid for having a child out of wedlock. Her mother had given her security and provided a nurturing environment for them. She held no shame over the humble life she shared with her mother.

Abigail clenched her hands in her lap. "How will my attendance garner any attention? I will but blend into the scenery."

"You misunderstood . . ." Lucas jumped from his seat and stalked to her side. He stood before Abigail, staring down at her, clearly unsure how to proceed.

Abigail raised her gaze, staring innocently into his. She sighed inwardly. Even when agitated, Lucas caused her heart to skip a beat. His eyes were ablaze, drilling into hers, demanding for her to understand what he attempted to say, without declaring what he truly thought. Lucas wanted to protect her feelings, but Abigail needed him to speak his mind. She needed to understand how he felt about her. If not, she would continue to pine away, hoping Lucas would confess his love for her. However, she must come to the reality of her wishful dreams meaning naught.

"Then please explain."

Lucas ran his hands through his hair in frustration. "Do you not understand the depth of your beauty? Every gentleman will fall at your feet once you step through the door. You are every man's fantasy with your curves and luxurious red hair. A goddess they would want to worship. Not to mention how your mind works, your sweet nature, and your innocence that enfolds you in a shield of protection. You are naughty and nice wrapped into a package that every gentleman will want to protect, no matter what his intentions are toward your virtue."

"Oh." Lucas's comments shocked Abigail into silence.

Lucas strode to the window. He needed to put distance between them before he drew Abigail into his arms. Her wide-eyed response undid him. He must leave or else he would be no better than the gentlemen he had described. His father had etched his betrothal to Selina Pemberton in stone before he could walk, let alone voice his opinion. The only offer he could make Abigail would wrap them in a lifetime of shame. She deserved to meet a gentleman who cared for her, and that was his father's purpose for giving her a season. Still, it didn't stop Lucas from wanting to deny her the chance for the same reason. He didn't want another man to love her.

"You never answered my question," Abigail stated.

He turned toward her. "Which question?"

"I suppose I have two questions now."

Lucas nodded for her to ask them.

Abigail twisted her fingers in her lap. "Do you perceive me as a servant's daughter?"

"Yes." Lucas shook his head at Abigail's gasp. "No. I mean no. You misunderstand."

Abigail rose and smoothed out her dress, clasping her hands in front of her. "No, I do not believe I have."

Lucas took a step forward before stopping. "Your other question."

"I no longer need to ask it. You have already answered the second question with your first answer. If you will excuse me, Lord Gray, I promised Gemma and Jacqueline my help in choosing their gowns for the musical this evening."

Lucas slumped into a chair at Abigail's departure. The full realization of how he had slandered Abigail's character overcame him. While he attempted to be gentle, he had allowed his own personal feelings for Abigail to become involved in his explanation. Their friendship of late had been rocky. Now he expected it to turn nonexistent. If he had thought to persuade her not to attend the season's functions, now he gave her every reason to go.

He only hoped she kept the reason for changing her mind to herself. Having Abigail upset with him was terrible enough. Once his cousins learned of his stupidity, he would need to seek refuge from their wrath.

He was a doomed man.

Chapter One

Abigail folded the letter, slid it back into the envelope, and laid it in her lap. Her destiny would take an alternative path if she followed through with the plans set forth in the missive. She would no longer be a concern for the Duke of Colebourne.

Or a hindrance for his son.

She released a deep sigh as she contemplated her choices. At the moment, thanks to her friendship, nay her family, her options were wide open. However, she felt if she accepted their offers, she would transfer the burden of her welfare from Colebourne to them. She wished to stay close to Gemma's side during the end of her pregnancy and help her with her newborn, but she must break the ties now. If not, then she would wander from one household to the next in pity, even though in her heart she knew her family didn't view their generosity in that sense. However, it would keep her from finding her own happiness.

Abigail snuggled deeper into the chair, wrapping the shawl tighter around her to ward off the chill. She should close the window she had opened, but she found comfort in the crisp air. It reminded her of the early morning walks she had taken with her mother before her mother started her workday. Not a day went by where she didn't miss her mother and the simplicity of the life they had led.

Her gaze traveled around the room, and part of her hoped it held the answers to her dilemma. Whenever she missed her mother, she found herself tucked away in the small parlor the duke had designed for his late wife. Abigail felt a kinship with the late duchess and the special parlor she had shared with the duke and their child. The space gave her the comfort of being part of their small family. Which was absurd since the very child was now a grown gentleman and a thorn in Abigail's side.

A thorn she loved with her whole heart.

Only he didn't care for her in the slightest. His actions over the past year proved so. At one time, they had held a special friendship, one they shared with no other. Their relationship had taken a turn for the worse once the duke set out to match his wards with the gentlemen of his choosing. She had come to understand how Lucas Gray viewed her. He thought her no more worthy than any of the other servants in the household.

Even though she wasn't a servant, since the Duke of Colebourne had raised her no differently than his nieces, Abigail never shook the turn in her standings. To her she would always be a member of the lower class, no matter how expensive of a gown she wore, the education the duke had provided for her, or the dowry Colebourne had set aside for her groom. And apparently Lucas viewed her in the same manner. Correction, she should address him as Lord Gray.

No, Abigail Cason was beneath his station and his every act since last spring proved what a fool she was to believe otherwise.

It came time to decide. Should she accept the offer Lord Ross had made of governing his two young daughters or remain at Colebourne Manor? If she remained, then she must accept that one fateful day she would have to bear witness to Lucas getting married and starting a family with a lady he chose as acceptable to his status. The constant reminder would crush her soul. So that reason alone made her decision easy. As much as it would hurt her to leave her family, it was the only option.

Lord Ross had shown his kindness by offering Abigail the position again when she couldn't accept it after the holidays. Colebourne had fallen ill after they returned from the Forresters, and she had stayed on to nurse him back to health. Now that he had recovered and granted her his permission, it was time for Abigail to respond to Lord Ross's request. He wanted her to start her new position immediately. He had traveled to London with his children, but the governess he hired had handed in her notice. The girl had apparently fallen in love with a shopkeeper after they arrived in London and was set to marry in a month's time. The governess had agreed to stay on until Abigail arrived.

Abigail only had one more promise to fulfill before she started a new beginning. The duke was holding a dinner to celebrate his success in finding matches for his nieces. The celebration to be held this weekend was the anniversary of when he started his matchmaking madness. A year ago, the duke held a house party that started a year full of scheming, manipulations, and more love than one could imagine possible. Her friends had found the other half of their souls, and Abigail found enjoyment from their unions. However, the dinner was only a bittersweet reminder of how the duke couldn't make a successful match between Abigail and Lucas.

She had promised Colebourne she wouldn't leave until the celebration was over. Then she would travel with the family to London, where they would start the season and she would start her new position. A fresh beginning to focus on, instead of dwelling on a lost love she never held a chance to begin with.

"There you are. I've been searching everywhere for you." Lucas strolled into the parlor and stood above her, capturing her attention with his demanding presence.

When he glanced at the letter on her lap, she covered her hand over it. "Does your father need me? He said he wanted to rest after luncheon before everybody started arriving."

Lucas's brows drew together. "Did you receive another letter from Selina? You two have come quite the bosom of friends."

"Yes, we have. However, the letter is not from Selina."

"Then it must be from Gemma." Lucas laughed. "She cannot wait until she arrives to share the latest gossip with you. No surprise since the two of you are inseparable."

Abigail cleared her throat. She had hoped to avoid this subject with Lucas until they departed for London. So, she attempted to inquire about the duke once again. "'Tis not from Gemma either. Does your father require my attention?"

Lucas frowned. Obviously, Abigail didn't want to tell him who the letter was from. But her secrecy of late only increased his curiosity to discover her plans for the future. He had selfish reasons for wanting Abigail to remain at Colebourne Manor, especially since all of his cousins had married and left to start their new lives. But this was Abby's home just as much as it was his. She belonged here, and it was his mission to make her see reason.

Since the letter wasn't from Gemma or Selina and she continued to keep it hidden, it must be from Lord Ross, the earl who tried to convince Abigail to become a governess to his children. Lucas knew little about the earl, except he resided in northern Scotland when not visiting London. In fact, few knew much about the esteemed Lord Ross. Only rumors and hearsay were speculated about the gentleman.

"No. He is still resting."

"Then is there something I can do for you, Lord Gray? Since you have searched the manor for me, it must be important."

Lucas sighed. "Must you continue with this Lord Gray business? I thought we came to a truce while caring for my father."

They had, but Abigail's heart cautioned her to keep an emotional distance from Lucas. If not, then she would wonder where she stood with him. His behavior the past year already made her question the strength of the bond of their friendship. She had misinterpreted it as love. Lucas had shown her a rare side of himself, and she had fooled herself into believing they stood a chance as a couple.

However, over the course of his cousins falling in love, he had shown his true character. He was a pompous, arrogant gentleman who shredded her heart to ribbons with his callous behavior. Now, with the course she set on the horizon, she needed to stay on guard. If not, he would ruin her for any other man.

However, this next week would be the last time she would spend in his company before she started the next chapter in her life. Didn't she owe it to herself to give him one more chance? Lord knows he didn't deserve it. But she longed for any opportunity to spend time in his company. Why ruin it with the past? One couldn't erase their actions; they could only move forward and hope the past didn't repeat itself. She wanted to give him a chance to redeem himself before she left. If not, then their friendship had all been for naught.

Abigail nodded. "We have. I apologize. Since your father has not requested my attention, I assumed you meant to lecture me on my future."

Lucas ran his hand through his hair in frustration. He had caused her to doubt and question his every action. His boorish behavior this past year had placed him in fragile standings with Abby. While he wanted to question her further about the letter she held, he knew it would only progress to him demanding she drop her foolish notions of becoming a servant. Which would lead to her stomping away and he would have to endure her silent treatment.

And right now, the news he had to share with her would only work to his advantage if he approached her differently. It was his only opportunity to convince Abigail to stay on. The circumstances couldn't have worked out any more perfectly. So, he chose to ignore her comment.

His smile held patience with her. "No. I have sought you out to inform you that the creek has washed out, delaying our guests' arrival."

Abigail sat forward, not realizing the letter dropped to the floor. "How horrible. Was anyone injured?"

"No. Thankfully, no one traveled on the road while it happened. I've sent men, and so has Sinclair, to stand guard, so no one tries to pass. They will redirect our guests to Sinclair's home until it is safe to make the travel to Colebourne Manor."

Abigail relaxed back into the chair. With a smirk, she addressed his remark. "Guests? Lucas, they are your family."

Lucas came alive with Abigail's smirk. Her teasing sparked the desire to kiss her sweet lips. However, he refrained as he always did. He refused to submit to the level of seducing an innocent miss. Even though it became more difficult with each day that passed.

"That they are." He groaned. "They are the bane of my existence."

Abigail threw a small pillow at him. "They are not. You love them dearly."

"Not as much as I love . . ." Lucas paused, shocked at what he had almost declared. He recovered quickly. "The peace and quiet of the manor with them not in residence."

Abigail had grown still when Lucas paused after he mentioned the word love. She rose abruptly, needing to put distance between them before she actually confessed her own love. "Yes. Well, you shall have your wish for a few extra days at least."

Lucas rose and moved closer to her. Abigail grew flustered when his breath brushed across her cheek as he reached up to tuck a stray curl behind her ear. She closed her eyes when his fingers swept across her cheek. Her heart started racing at the gentle gesture.

Lucas bent his head to whisper. "I hope during their delay we can fill our days as we once used to."

Abigail gulped. "As in?"

"A game or two of chess and some walks through the garden. Perhaps our usual debate of well-written poetry versus the works of the utter rubbish you call romance," he teased her as his fingers trailed along her neck.

Abigail's eyes flew open. "Do you not mean the works of true poets?"

"No, love. You know perfectly well what I meant." He brushed his thumb across her lip, forgetting the promise he had made to himself about not touching her.

Abigail's mouth opened at his touch, and her tongue struck out to wet her dry lips but only ended up licking his thumb. Lucas's gaze grew dark at her innocent act, and he stepped closer. The heat from his body wrapped her in a warm embrace, making her ache for his arms to circle her and take away the remaining chill separating them. When he lowered his head, Abigail panicked and stepped to the side.

She hurried to the door, fighting against her desire to allow him to kiss her. "If the guests are not arriving, then I must speak with Mrs. Oakes on the meals."

Lucas lowered his head and winced at what he had almost attempted. He had been about to kiss Abigail. He had no excuse except when her tongue stroked across his thumb, he lost all rational thought and only wished to indulge in his fantasy.

"Abigail," he started to apologize, but the letter she dropped caught his attention. He bent to retrieve it and noted the return address as one Lord Ross. "You cannot still be contemplating the role of governess," Lucas demanded.

Abigail paused and turned at the harsh tone from Lucas. He was holding the letter from Lord Ross. She must have dropped it when he distracted her with his attention. Abigail stalked back toward him, her desire quickly vanishing into fury. "I am not only contemplating, but I have accepted Lord Ross's offer. I shall start my position once we travel to London. You will not have to suffer embarrassment this season with my attendance at your social gatherings. Instead, I shall be performing duties in my actual place. The place of a servant in a house of a lord of the ton."

She reached for the letter, but Lucas grabbed her wrist with his other hand. Even in her frustration, her skin tingled from his touch. Her body betrayed her with its desire to have him wrap her in his arms and kiss away every obstacle in their path to be together.

"You misconstrue my intentions."

"I do not. You have made yourself clear as day on how you view me. Also, it is not of your concern about how I live my life." She tugged her arm away and snatched the letter from his hand.

Lucas growled. "You are the most exasperating lady I have ever known."

Abigail glared at Lucas. "Well, we shall just have to add that trait to your list about my character."

She held no clue how he regarded her. He knew the ins and outs to the depth of her character more than anyone else. Even now when she stood in front of him in a fury, she possessed a gracefulness like no other lady. Her fiery gaze darkened to a lush green forest full of mysterious danger. His own desire heightened as her body stood poised to attack. Abigail's breasts heaved with each aggravated breath she drew and her nipples tightened under his bold stare. He wanted to drag her into his arms and kiss the snarl from her lips. Instead of acting out his desires, he continued to provoke her anger.

"I will also list how naïve you are to consider working for a gentleman that no one has ever heard of before," Lucas taunted her.

"Lord Ross is a noble gentleman with strong Scottish ties," Abigail argued.

"And who offered this bit of knowledge?"

A smug smile spread across Abigail's face. "Your father."

Lucas narrowed his gaze. "Exactly. You have proven my point."

Abigail stepped forward and jabbed her finger into Lucas's chest. With each point she declared, her finger pressed in harder. "The only item proven today is your insufferable need to direct my life. The second is your overbearing conceited arrogance. And finally, you wished you held an ounce of integrity as Lord Ross holds. He has shown nothing but generosity with his offer, not to mention his kind regard when we correspond. You could learn a lot from Lord Ross about how to treat a lady. Oh, I apologize, I mean a servant." Abigail snarled her last comment before storming out of the parlor.

Lucas watched Abigail leave, rubbing his chest from where she had touched him. He tried to soak up the scorching heat, but it disappeared as quickly as the lady herself. And he did regard her as a lady, one so fine no other could compare. He might have riled her temper and caused himself more trouble with his damaging comments, but it was worth it to experience her touch.

Lucas shook his head. He had finally fallen into the depths of madness his family suffered from. Now he wondered how he would ever pull himself out.

Or did he want to?

Chapter Two

"I see you still have not mastered diplomacy." Colebourne sauntered inside the parlor. He sat down in his favorite chair by the window.

Lucas scowled. "Your interference is not needed, Father."

Colebourne sighed. "I agree."

Lucas swung his gaze to his father. "You agree? Have you fallen ill again or is this another twist to your manipulations?"

Colebourne smiled at his son with a patience he had used on the boy when Lucas was younger and always getting into mischief. Since then, Lucas had grown into a gentleman to make a father proud. However, through the years, the boy had lost his sense of mischief and turned into a stuffed-shirt proper gentleman who allowed the rules of society to dictate his life. Those same rules kept him from declaring his love for the lady who had stomped from the parlor in a huff.

Colebourne had hoped Lucas would come to his senses concerning the lass. Instead, he made his relationship with Abigail worse off than before the holidays. During Colebourne's recovery, the two had come to a truce of sorts, but it appeared as if his son had broken the delicate connection this afternoon.

"No. I am perfectly fit. I have decided to stop interfering with you and Abigail because I now see the error of my ways. It would be a mistake on my part to force a match between you and Abigail."

"Finally."

Colebourne continued, watching his son with skepticism. "Yes. It was wrong of me to force you into another union not of your choosing. After your betrothal to Selina ended, I should have stopped. You should have the same option of choosing your own bride as I had when I chose your mother. A lady who fits in with your standing in society and who will not embarrass you with her lowly beginnings. A lady who will listen to your word and not argue her stand. It is not fair of me to saddle you with a bride who doesn't share your values or outlook on life."

Colebourne paused, expecting Lucas to make an objection. When Lucas didn't, he continued. "Nor is it fair to Abigail. She deserves a gentleman who loves her for the lovely soul she is. I only hope you make a wise choice and it will not cause any sort of disruption in our family."

Lucas had started pacing during his father's speech. While his father sounded sincere, he didn't quite believe a word he spoke. His father could spin a yard as well as the most polished politician. However, his father displayed not a hint of deviousness. He appeared to speak the truth and Lucas took him at his word. Only the comments of him not playing matchmaker, the other comments his father spoke were false.

"Thank you for not interfering with my decision to not pursue Abigail as a bride. I am glad that you finally see reason, no matter how mistaken you are in my objections."

Colebourne's brows drew together in confusion. "How so?"

Lucas started pacing again as he made his points valid. "First of all, Abigail is the finest of all the ladies in England. I would only hold honor if she were to become my bride. Second, she has more grace and beauty than those vultures who call themselves my peers. Abigail puts them to shame. Also, I hold her opinion on all matters with respect. She makes valid points with her arguments, unlike those other silly debutantes who, heaven forbid, have a thought of their own."

Lucas stopped before his father and glared at him. "And for my last objection, I love her for the lovely soul she is. No other gentleman is as worthy of her as I am."

Colebourne clapped his hands together. "Excellent. What is your course of action to persuade her to forgive your ill attempts at acting a gentleman? You must hurry and profess your love soon. We leave for London in two weeks, and she plans on accepting the post with Lord Ross."

Lucas stared at his father in disbelief. "I am not asking Abigail to marry me, nor am I professing my love. Whatever gave you that assumption?"

"Why, you. Only a few seconds ago, you professed your love and how wonderful of a wife Abigail would be for you."

Lucas turned away, running his hands through his hair. His father had done it again. He had provoked him into confessing his affections for Abigail by pretending indifference to Lucas's choice for a bride. The conniving old man. He didn't know who was more exasperating today. Abigail or his father.

"You are mistaken once again. I only stated how I viewed Abigail. It by no means was my declaration of undying love or of a proposal to come. Also, what is your intention in providing Abigail with false information on Lord Ross's character?"

"I provided no false information. I have corresponded with Lord Ross myself and find him to be an honorable fellow worthy of gaining Abigail as a governess," Colebourne stated.

"On what standards?" Lucas questioned.

Colebourne folded his hands in his lap. "On the fact of his devotion to his daughters. He cares for their welfare by providing them with the care worthy of his love by hiring Abigail. Lord Ross provided me with his promise of allowing Abigail time off whenever someone needs her. He understands her connection to our family and supports keeping the ties bonded."

Lucas scoffed. "A regular commendable gentleman he is."

"Yes, I believe he is. Who knows, maybe he will fall in love with our Abigail," Colebourne baited his son.

Lucas snarled. "Never."

Colebourne shrugged. "An act out of our control. Only fate will decide."

Lucas shook his head. "Fate? Now, I know you have recovered. You are still as maddening as ever."

"It is much better to be mad than an arrogant arse who with each passing day proves he is unworthy of a certain lady's love."

Lucas didn't even bother to reply to his father's taunts and stormed out of the parlor. As much as he wanted to deny his love for Abigail, his father spoke the truth. But it was the depth of his love that stopped him from pursuing her. If he would, then she would endure a lifetime of whispers behind her back, shunned at every event they attended, shamed just because she had been born to a servant. No matter how much her mother and his family loved her, it wouldn't erase her humble beginnings. He would endure a lifetime of never experiencing their love for Abigail to never suffer from another person's slander.

Not even understanding how his rejection hurt her more deeply than any act by another person.

~~~~~~~

"Your Grace?"

"Yes, Oakes."

The butler frowned at the duke. "Per your instructions, I had the guests diverted to Lord Sinclair's home. I have a message from Lady Forrester."

Colebourne held out his hand for the missive. "Excellent. Now we must keep Lucas and Abigail away from the road by any means necessary."

Oakes nodded. "Also, I informed the servants of the plot. They wish for me to convey their desire to assist you in any way they are capable of."

Colebourne laughed. "The most devoted of servants. Tell the lot I will appreciate any assistance given. But they must do so without Lucas or Abigail becoming suspicious."

"I will relay the message. Is there anything else you require?"

"Yes, inform Mrs. Oakes that I shall dine in my bedchamber this evening." He winked at Oakes.

Oakes smiled. "Very well, Your Grace." He bowed and left the duke alone to read his letter and finish plotting his latest match.

Colebourne opened Susanna's message.

Theodore,

What a marvelous decision to route the guests to Charlie & Jasper's home. We will settle in here until you send word for us to arrive. I hope during this delay, Lucas and Abigail will set their stubbornness to the side and admit how much they care for one another. I know how much you want them to find their happily ever after together.

If they still haven't connected once we arrive, then I, along with the rest of the family, will attempt the impossible. And if we cannot, then we must accept what is not meant to be. We owe it to Lucas and Abigail to respect their wishes. However, that time has yet to happen.All is fair in love and war, my cohort.

The madness of our matchmaking will prevail.

Your faithful co-conspirator,

Susanna

Colebourne chuckled. "I can always count on your lovely sister," he spoke to the image sitting across from him.

Olivia shook her head at his ploys. But the mischievous grin lighting her face spoke of her approval. His son would call him mad for speaking to his mother as if she were present. But over the years, he had sought comfort from their imaginary visits. Their secret conversations kept him sane while raising Lucas and his wards.

"I promise you, Livvy, I will succeed and make a match between Lucas and Abigail."

"I know you will, my love." Olivia's whisper floated away with her memory.

Chapter Three

Lucas searched every possible hiding spot Abigail sought when trying to avoid him but came up empty. He had already checked with her maid, Polly, and she hadn't seen her either. Which only left the kitchens. Abigail would retreat there whenever troubled. She had told him she felt the most comfortable amongst the servants, who were also her friends. He had told her how absurd that was, but now he understood her reasons.

He walked through the kitchens but didn't see her about. However, the aroma of freshly baked biscuits beckoned him toward the tray holding a plate with a pot of tea. He reached out to grab a handful when Cook slapped his hand.

"Those are not for you, Lord Gray."

Lucas turned his most charming smile on the older woman who always spoiled him with his favorite treats. "Ahh, Cook, I only want to sample a few before tea." He winked at her when she kept frowning at him with her disapproval. "You make the most mouthwatering morsels in the county. Do I see cherries in them?"

Cook humphed. "County? I do not even hold the honor of all of England? I can see why you have ruffled the miss's feathers," she muttered under her breath.

He opened his mouth to question her further, but Polly and Douglas, a footman, walked into the kitchen. They didn't see him at first standing behind Cook, but once they noticed, Polly dipped into a curtsy and Douglas bowed.

"Lord Gray." Polly glared at him.

Douglas's eyes widened at Polly's tone, but he addressed Lucas in the same manner. "Lord Gray."

Lucas frowned. While they addressed him properly, it was unusual, considering how his father kept a relaxed atmosphere with the servants. To his father, they were hardworking and deserved the same respect. So whenever no visitors were present, everyone addressed one another on a first-name basis. They were only to address them as lord and lady when guests arrived for a visit.

"Douglas, please gather the tray. Abigail is ready for the small respite." Polly directed the footman out of the kitchen.

Lucas shook his head at the bizarre behavior. "I noticed there was only one cup on the tray. May I have another to join Abigail for tea? And perhaps another plate of biscuits."

Cook pinched her lips at his request and slammed a mug on the table, one the servants drank from, not from the set on the tray. Instead of gathering another plate, she moved away from him and pulled out a potato from a bowl to chop.

"Biscuits?" he reminded her.

She quirked a brow at him. "I made those for the miss. Cherry biscuits are her favorite."

"I know they are. They are mine, too." He tried his charming smile on her again. But like earlier, he failed to coax a smile from her.

"I apologize, my lord. I have none to give you."

If Lucas knew any differently, he would think the servants conspired against him. Which was ridiculous. He couldn't think of anything he'd done to earn their dislike. When Cook continued to ignore him, he sauntered away. On his way to find Abigail, each servant he passed regarded him with either *my lord* or *Lord Gray*. However, his luck took a turn for the better when he overheard Douglas commenting to Mrs. Oakes on where Abigail took her tea. He started off toward the library when Mrs. Oakes stopped him.

"Lord Gray?"

Lucas paused. "Yes, Mrs. Oakes."

"May I see you in my office? There is something I wish to address with you." She swept her hand toward her office.

He nodded and followed on her heels. Once he entered, she closed the door and took a seat behind her desk. She regarded him with a shrewd look that made Lucas want to squirm. It reminded him of every lecture she had delivered to him in his youth whenever he ruined a servant's work with his hijinks. With her guidance, he had learned how valuable a person's pride was and how to respect one's value, no matter their hierarchy in life. His gut tightened to think he had disappointed her.

When she slid a tin wrapped in a ribbon across the desk at him, he grew even more confused. She nodded at him to take it. He lifted the tin and noted the candymaker from the village stamped on the lid. "What is this for?" he asked.

"To help you," Mrs. Oakes answered.

"Help me with what exactly?"

"In winning Miss Abigail's forgiveness."

Lucas quirked a brow. "Do I need assistance?"

Mrs. Oakes nodded. "Yes. And not only with Miss Abigail. If you require a warm fire for bed, a seasoned dinner, not to mention any other service, then you must make amends with the dear girl."

Lucas blew out a breath and slumped into a chair. "I take it from the cold regard I received in the kitchen that all the servants have taken Abigail's side."

The housekeeper tsked her disapproval. "It has nothing to do with taking sides. You have upset them with the way you have treated Abigail of late. May I speak bluntly with you, Lord Gray?"

He threw his hands in the air. "You too with the Lord Gray?"

"Lucas." She lowered her voice for him to focus his attention on the matter at hand.

He sighed. "Yes."

"Over the years, I have watched you grow into an outstanding gentleman. Your patience with your cousins and the friendship you hold with Abigail would have made your mother very proud. I know it has your father. However, ever since your cousins have gotten married, you have grown possessive of Abigail. So much so that you confuse her with your intentions. You will not admit your affections, yet you keep every available gentleman away from her. I will not discipline you on how you have treated her regarding her status in society. I believe you will torture yourself enough once you realize how you have spoken out of turn. Am I correct?" Mrs. Oakes inquired. Lucas nodded.

Mrs. Oakes leaned forward to deliver her ultimatum. "Until you decide to treat Abigail as the fine lady she is, you will meet resistance from the servants. As much as your family regards her as one of them, the servants feel the same. That girl deserves the moon and the stars, and if you will not give those to her, then you must stand aside for her to follow the path she chooses. In the meantime, I believe if you offer her a token of forgiveness, she might accept your apology."

Lucas sat for a few moments, contemplating what she said. If he were any other lord, he would reprimand her for her insolence. However,

Mrs. Oakes was more than a housekeeper; she was a mother figure to him. He respected her opinions, even the ones that dealt with the heart. As much as he wished he could inform her of his plans to pursue Abigail as his bride, he couldn't. He had made himself a promise, and even though it grew more difficult to keep, he must resist his feelings for Abigail.

"Toffee?" he asked.

Mrs. Oakes smiled. "Yes."

He said no more and rose to leave. When he reached the door, he turned with a frown. "I thought the creek washed out the road."

Mrs. Oakes's hands fluttered around with the papers on her desk, and she wouldn't meet his gaze. "Oh, Mr. Oakes bought those for me a few days ago. I thought they would be more beneficial to you than to my hips." She offered him a timid smile.

He shook the tin. "Wish me luck."

"No luck is needed. We both know once you offer Abigail a charming smile and a few smooth words, she will forgive you. It is how you choose to move forward where I wish you luck."

~~~~~~

Lucas peered around the doorframe, watching Abigail snuggle under a throw while reading a book. She grabbed a biscuit to nibble on after she turned the page. He kept staring as he worked up his courage to approach her. She appeared content and at peace, and if he showed himself, it would draw a frown upon her lovely features and set her on guard. He wished to repair their friendship, and for that miracle to happen, he must stay quiet on his opinion no matter how wrong he thought she was.

"Here goes nothing," he muttered before strolling into the library.

He stood in front of her, but Abigail didn't raise her head to acknowledge him. She kept on eating the biscuits and reading. When she kept flipping the pages after a few seconds, he knew his presence agitated her. He smirked when he realized she didn't read a single word, betraying her act of indifference. Lucas rocked on his heels with pleasure.

Abigail fought to rein in her annoyance. Lucas Gray was the most irritating gentleman in all of England. Yet her heart refused to acknowledge his disreputable behavior. She longed for the days when they were only Lucas and Abby who held a unique friendship. Where they could be themselves, and the pressure from the outside world never rock the foundation of what they held dear. It wasn't Lucas's fault how their lives had changed over the course of the past year. Nor should the blame of her tortured heart lie at his feet.

He had never given her any promises of everlasting love. It was only a few months ago when his father had kept his promise to the Duke of Norbury for Lucas to marry the duke's daughter. However, Selina Pemberton had married Lucas's cousin Duncan Forrester, breaking the betrothal and freeing him to find his own bride. It wasn't his fault Lucas found her lacking. If he didn't, he would have stolen a kiss or two. No. That act would be too improper for the marquess. Heaven forbid he should ruin his reputation for the likes of her. He made his opinion clear about how he only viewed her as a lowly servant. A bruise to her ego to imagine she meant more in his eyes.

However, it no longer mattered. She would set her own course and Lucas Gray be damned. Oh, who did she fool? Even now, with his boyish behavior before her, he captured her attention, refusing to disappear. No matter how hard she wished for him to. She kept turning the pages, not capturing a word. Perhaps Lucas would leave her at peace if she acknowledged him.

She raised her head, but before she could question his presence, he thrust a tin in her face. Not just any tin, but one filled with toffee, her favorite treat. Her mouth watered for a piece. Her gaze slid upward and met his lopsided smile, and his eyes begged for forgiveness. Abigail found herself lost once again in Lucas's powerful force. She reached for the tin, but he pulled it back.

"I am offering an exchange as well as an apology. My behavior earlier was uncalled for," Lucas apologized.

Abigail nodded. She didn't want to disagree with Lucas anymore today. "You offer me a token of an apology, yet you wish for something in return. I do not see the fairness of your suggestion."

Lucas twisted his lips to the side as he pondered her comment. "You are correct, my friend. How rude of me to suggest such a trade." He sighed. "'Tis I only wish for some of your cherry biscuits that Cook made."

Abigail winced, glancing at the empty plate. "I am afraid I have eaten them all."

Lucas followed her gaze and saw only a few measly crumbs remained on the plate. "Perhaps you might share the toffee." He handed her the tin and sat on the sofa next to her.

Abigail laughed at his dejected expression. "I will share both, *my friend*." She emphasized the endearment to let him know she forgave him. As she always did and always would.

Lucas's frown disappeared at Abigail's twinkling laughter. The soft melody clung to his tortured soul. As much as he appeared the arrogant arse, he suffered as greatly as Abigail did. His unrequited love kept them apart. "You cannot. Cook said there were no biscuits left."

Abigail drew her hand up to her mouth to hide her chuckle. "There is plenty left unless she fed a small traveling party between when we baked them this morning to now."

"Not that I am aware of. However, Cook was adamant that none remained for me to enjoy."

Abigail cleared her throat and looked away instead of facing her guilt. She had vented while baking this morning about how inconsiderate Lucas's comments were since Colebourne had started his matchmaking madness. It appeared Cook set out to punish Lucas by withholding one of his favorite treats. She needed to make this right. While she held much irritation with the marquess, she didn't want the servants to treat him differently. Their disagreements were between them and no one else.

She set the tin in his lap. "Please hold this for a second."

She rose and walked out of the library, searching for a footman. Once she located one, she conveyed her message and returned to the library. She sat next to Lucas on the sofa and gazed at his fingers as he toyed with the ribbon wrapped around the tin. What sensation would he stir inside her if he stroked her body? Would it be as gentle? She shook her head to clear her thoughts.

Lucas rattled the tin. "Shall we?"

Abigail smiled at his impatience. "No."

"Why ever not? I know your mouth is watering to savor a bite."

Abigail shrugged. "Perhaps."

Lucas tugged on the ribbon, untying the knot.

"Lucas," Abigail warned.

He pulled the ribbon apart and tied it around Abigail's wrist. His thumb lingered, brushing back and forth against the rapid fluttering of her pulse. Abigail held her breath at the exquisite caress.

"Make a wish," Lucas whispered.

Abigail shook her head. He tempted her with a silly game they played when they were younger.

Lucas turned a devastating smile on her, weakening her resolve. "Pretty please, for me."

"'Tis a silly tradition. We are too old to make wishes that will never come true."

Lucas circled Abigail's wrist and tugged her closer. He bent his head to whisper in her ear. "Humor me, Abby." His warm breath teased her senses. "Close your eyes." Abigail followed his direction. "Now I have one simple rule for this wish."

"Wishes are not to be dictated by rules," Abigail argued.

Lucas closed his own eyes, inhaling her flowery scent. If he didn't divert his gaze, he would defy his resistance. He ached to trail his lips along her neck and kiss every delectable inch of her.

He laughed at her logic. "They are if I deem them so."

He couldn't help himself, and his hand stroked up her arm and back down again to circle her wrist.

Abigail's breath caught at his caress. "Very well. What is your rule?"

She knew exactly what she wanted to wish, even though it would never come true. But her body begged for him to speak his rule.

"Your wish can only be what you wish to happen today. Nothing for the future. Only for the here and now."

Abigail moved her hand to untie the ribbon. Her fingers entangled with his. "I wish for . . ." She silently finished her wish as she pulled at the bow.

The ribbon fluttered to the floor and their gazes locked. Neither one looked away. The passion swirling around the room captured them in its whirlwind. Time stood still, waiting for one of them to act.

"Here you go, miss, more cherry biscuits." Polly interrupted them, carrying a tray. "Cook sent you a fresh pot of tea too."

Lucas jumped up from the settee and strode toward the fireplace. He saw a warm blush spread across Abigail's cheeks when she responded to Polly. He wasn't the only one affected by the charge in the air.

"Thank you, Polly. And give my thanks to Cook."

Polly glared in his direction. "Sorry, miss. I thought you were alone."

"Lord Gray has joined me for tea."

"Humph," Polly muttered before leaving.

Abigail frowned after the maid. "I apologize for Polly's rude behavior."

Lucas ran his hand through his hair. "It would appear I have fallen on the wrong side of the servants' graces."

Abigail cringed. "I fear that is my fault."

"How so?"

"I might have vented my frustration at your highhandedness while baking with Cook this morning." Abigail held out the plate of biscuits as a peace offering.

Lucas grabbed the treat and took a bite, moaning at how delicious it was. "Nothing I do not deserve."

Abigail poured him a cup of tea and added his two sugars, stirring it before handing it over. "Still, it was inappropriate for me to discuss my frustrations. I will refrain in the future by biting my tongue."

Lucas laughed, grabbing a handful of biscuits. "No need for such drastic measures, my dear. They taste marvelous."

Abigail took a bite of one and moaned, agreeing. There was much for them to say, but the peacefulness hovering around them kept her from dwelling on the strain in their relationship.

Soon, Lucas had her laughing at his silliness, taking her back to a time when this was the norm for them. They spent the afternoon reading and talking. They finished the biscuits and half of the tin of toffee. Perhaps friendship was all destiny meant for them. When the dinner bell rang, they both rose and bumped into each other.

Lucas reached out and steadied her. His hand lingered. "Abigail."

Her eyes lifted. "Lucas."

He brushed his thumb across a stray crumb near her lips and lowered his head to kiss her. Lucas no longer wanted to fight the attraction simmering between them. He only wanted to indulge in one kiss. Then, hopefully, he would regain his sanity.

Abigail panicked. Even though she had dreamed of this day, she feared he would regret his action. And she couldn't handle any more of his rejection. So, she fled before he could act upon his intention. She would rather die aching for a taste of his lips than see his eyes cloud with revulsion for kissing someone below his station.

"Abigail," Lucas called after her.

She left him. He was about to kiss her and she fled. Was he mistaken in the desire that flared in her gaze? All afternoon her gaze had never strayed far from him, devouring him. It was agony to sit so near her and watch her tongue lick her lips with each bite she took. He ached for her tongue to lick his lips. She left him before he could act out his wish for the day. Even though it was Abigail's wish to make, he had made his own.

Lucas lowered his head and caught sight of the ribbon lying on the floor. He reached down to pick it up. He slid it between his thumb and finger and could have sworn the heat from her skin singed his fingers.

"Lord Gray," Oakes addressed him from the door.

Lucas shoved the ribbon in his pocket. "Yes, Oakes."

"Your father is in need of more rest and is taking dinner in his bedchamber this evening. So, it shall only be you and Miss Abigail for dinner."

Perhaps his wish might get granted after all. "Then direct Mrs. Oakes to set a small table in my mother's parlor. We will serve ourselves. The servants may have an early evening to spend at their leisure."

"Very well, my lord."

Lucas's grin widened at the turn of his evening. Instead of making polite conversation with his father and Abigail, he would get to enjoy a more intimate setting with the lady who set his heart aflame.

Lucas felt himself falling victim to the madness of love.

Chapter Four

Abigail followed Oakes along the dark hallway. Only the glow from the candlestick he held lit their way. An empty table met her when she arrived for dinner. Oakes had informed her the duke was taking his dinner in his bedchamber for an early evening. Abigail had tried to check on the duke, but Oakes assured her Colebourne was well. Then he'd told her to follow him. Once they reached the small parlor, Oakes wished her a good evening and took himself off.

Abigail stepped into her comforting sanctuary to find it aglow with a dozen lit candles. Lucas stood near a small table, holding a single red rose. Since their guests never arrived, Abigail had chosen not to change her clothing. And to her relief, neither had Lucas. He had even discarded his suit coat and cravat.

Lucas stepped forward and handed Abigail the rose. She drew it to her face and breathed in the heavenly fragrance. Her fingers stroked over the soft petals and she smiled at Lucas's kind gesture. "Thank you."

"You are welcome." He guided her to the table and pulled out a chair.

Abigail laid the rose on the table. "Why are we dining in here?"

Lucas settled across from Abigail. "I am still redeeming myself. Since Father was not joining us, I did not want to sit across from you at the enormous dining table. I thought you would enjoy eating our dinner in your favorite room."

"What a wonderful idea. I know it is silly, but I find such comfort in this parlor."

"It is not silly. My mother found the same comfort. I remember her and Father enjoying many meals together in here." Lucas smiled fondly at Abigail.

Abigail reached out and squeezed his hand. She heard the sorrow of missing his mother. "They were a lovely couple. I remember the first time I met your mother. Gemma's parents allowed me to come along with my mother while they visited Colebourne Manor."

Her gaze traveled across the room, landing on the chair in the corner. "We were playing hide and seek and I snuck in here to hide behind that chair." She pointed at the chair. "Before I knew it, your mother came into the parlor and started reading. I don't remember how much time passed, but it felt like forever. I started to cry from the fear of getting my mother in trouble. Your mother heard me and coaxed me out of my hiding spot. Then she gathered me on her lap and read to me. In between reading, she asked me silly questions to calm me down. After that occasion, your mother would always seek me out to talk."

Lucas stared at her in surprise. "I never knew that."

"Why would you? You were a playful little boy who always terrorized us with your mischief," Abigail teased.

"You make me out to have been a holy terror."

Abigail arched an eyebrow. "Were you not?"

Lucas laughed. "I was. However, in my defense, I grew out of my boyish need for trouble."

A solemn expression settled on Abigail's face. "Yes, you have. You are now the ever proper gentleman who abides by the rules and structures of society. Quite the opposite boy from your youth."

"There is nothing wrong with leading a structured life. It gives one a sense of purpose to achieve the goals they set forth for themselves," Lucas attempted to defend himself, but even he fell flat with his argument.

"You are very correct. Now what has Cook prepared for us to dine on this evening?" Abigail lifted the cover on her plate.

Lucas frowned for a brief second. He sensed Abigail was deflecting an argument. Did she find him lacking because he disagreed with his family's improper behavior of late? His family needed someone sensible to look after their affairs with their unstableness.

He lifted his own cover to see it full of cherry-filled biscuits. Abigail giggled at the sight, and he had to chuckle along. It appeared Cook forgave him. "I guess I am enjoying a dinner filled with sugar."

"If you promise me a walk in the garden after dinner, it might help to persuade me to share my meal with you."

Lucas looked at the platter filled with enough food to feed two people. "Only if you share mine too."

Abigail held out her hand. "Deal."

Lucas shook her hand. He wanted to keep holding it and soak up her warmth. However, he didn't wish to make her uncomfortable. The dinner he planned for this evening was only the start of repairing their friendship. And perhaps the start of a seduction.

Abigail rose and slid her chair closer to his and set the plate between them while Lucas poured them each a glass of wine. Throughout the meal, they settled back into the comfortable friendship they had earlier in the library. It was as if the past year had never happened. Every single conceited argument Lucas had subjected Abigail to vanished into thin air.

After eating another round of biscuits, Lucas leaned back in his chair, moaning. "I fear I will never look longingly at another cherry biscuit again."

Abigail moaned too and rubbed her stomach. "Hopefully that was the last of them."

Lucas rose, holding out his hand. "Come, my dear. Let us enjoy a stroll through the garden before the evening grows much later."

"I will need to gather my shawl."

"Nonsense. You can wear my suit coat to ward off the chill." Lucas held out his coat.

"But you will freeze," Abigail argued.

As long as he was anywhere near Abigail, freezing wasn't an option. Her very nearness set his soul on fire. "I will survive."

Abigail accepted the coat as Lucas settled it over her shoulders. "If you insist."

"I do." He guided her outside.

At his request, Oakes had lit lanterns throughout the garden for them. He hoped he had slid back into the servants' good graces again. Because he didn't know how to survive if they turned on him, too. Over the past year, he had angered his cousins by his treatment of Abigail. He didn't understand why they couldn't accept his reasoning. He only tried to keep Abigail from getting hurt.

Abigail didn't know what to make of this evening or the day, for that matter. Lucas continued to make amends with his thoughtful gestures. Even now, he guided her along the path, keeping her out of harm's way in the darkness. The glow from the lanterns only allowed so much light to escape. While it gave them a sense of security, it also highlighted the secrecy kept hidden in the shadows.

They stopped near Abigail's favorite tree in the garden. The weeping willow's branches rustled in the soft breeze. While the tree always appeared sad, this evening it danced with a lightness that Abigail felt herself. Lucas grabbed a branch and tickled the leaves against her arm. She smiled at his teasing gesture. There still lurked a mischievous boy who defied all the odds against him hidden under his proper exterior. Perhaps they had a chance if she could draw him out to play once again.

Abigail tipped her head to gaze at the sky. It was a clear night, and the stars twinkled above her, daring her to make a bold gesture. As much as she goaded Lucas on acting as the proper gentleman, she was no different. Because of her standing in society, Abigail walked the fine line of proper decorum. She never wanted to give Colebourne any reason to find fault in her character.

A star shot across the sky and started free-falling. Abigail grabbed Lucas's arm, pointing at the sky. "Hurry, now it is your turn to make a wish."

Lucas glanced up at the shooting star. He closed his eyes and reopened them to see the hopeful expression on Abigail's face. He needed no other encouragement. Lucas deliberately backed Abigail up against the tree.

"Lucas?"

He placed his finger against her soft lips. "Shh."

"What did you wish for?" Abigail whispered.

"I wished for . . ." Lucas lowered his head.

If ever a girl wished for her first kiss to be in a romantic setting with the knight of her dreams, then Abigail became that girl on this magical night. Her first kiss was everything she imagined it to be and more.

Lucas brushed his mouth slowly across her lips. Once. Twice. On the third pass, his tongue stroked her mouth to open. Abigail gasped at the bold caress, and he captured the sound with a kiss, declaring his desire. He pulled her into his embrace and ravished her mouth with a need only Abigail understood. What started out as a sweet kiss swiftly turned into something Abigail had only ever read about.

With each sweep of his tongue across hers, Abigail fell deeper in love with Lucas. He dominated her senses with his need. She wrapped her arms around his neck and clung to him, his jacket slipping from her shoulders and falling to the ground. Their sighs whispered in the night air, singing the passion that flared between them.

Lucas had tasted no lips sweeter than Abigail's. The kiss was more perfect than he ever imagined it to be. No fantasy could compare to drowning in her kiss in this moment. He stroked his tongue inside her mouth, savoring the flavor of cherries. He brought his hands up to cup her face, trying to get himself under control. Lucas drew his lips away with much reluctance and pressed his forehead against hers, drawing in a ragged breath.

"Wishes really do come true," she whispered in awe.

Lucas traced his thumb across her lips. "Yes, they do," he whispered in return.

Abigail gasped once she realized what she had confessed. She pulled out of his grasp and hurried away. She stopped a few feet away and turned slightly. "Thank you for a magical evening. I hope your wish comes true like mine did." Then she rushed toward the house.

Lucas watched Abigail dash away and wondered if she left because he had overstepped his bounds or because the attraction simmering between them had unleashed itself. He hoped he didn't scare her away. If so, he would have to start fresh again tomorrow. They only had a couple of days left to themselves before his family descended on them. A short amount of time to convince Abigail how he felt about her.

He bent to retrieve his coat and held it to his face. Lucas breathed in her flowery scent and wondered if his valet wouldn't think it too strange for him to keep it from getting cleaned. With a spring to his step, he followed Abigail back to the manor. Before he stepped inside, he glanced at the sky. The stars winked their approval of his kiss down at him.

He spoke to the surrounding silence. "It more than came true, Abigail. You granted my wish with your whisper-soft sighs and the sweetness of your kiss."

Chapter Five

"I hope your father has not taken a turn for the worse again," Abigail stated as they walked along the open fields.

"No. I believe he is reserving his energy for when everyone arrives."

Lucas sensed his father had made himself scarce to force Abigail and him to spend time with one another. He was forever playing matchmaker. It had taken Lucas awhile, but he now understood his father's agenda. Duncan and Selina's marriage showed how the power of love defied all odds when one held faith.

His cousin and ex-betrothed never once allowed doubt to enter into their union. Selina had fought against the union because of the pressure her father placed her under to fulfill a promise made in the past. Also, Selina had been unsure of Duncan's true intentions. But once they confessed their love, nothing had stood in their way. Unlike Lucas, who allowed other people's opinions to hold him hostage in pursuing Abigail.

"'Tis probably for the best, considering we leave for London soon."

Lucas bit his tongue. London was a sore subject between them, and he didn't want to ruin the afternoon with his comments. "I agree."

Abigail waited for Lucas to state his opinion again about her plans once they reached London, but he stayed silent. She wondered if he had accepted her becoming a governess or if he saved his argument for when everyone arrived, so someone else would take his side. However, it would

be a pointless attempt because Abigail had already convinced everyone else
and they offered their unwavering support. Even though they all offered her
other alternatives to keep her close, they understood her need to strike out
on her own.

Neither one of them had mentioned the kiss they shared the previous
evening. A kiss forever fixated in her memories. Who knew a kiss opened
the door to another's soul? It was more than a simple kiss two souls shared.
It was a testament to the powerful connection that bonded them as one. Oh,
the fantasies she had repressed the past year flared to life again. Her dreams
of them getting married and raising a family at Colebourne Manor
flourished. She pictured little boys with light brown hair and hazel eyes,
smiling their father's charming smile as they made excuses for their
mischief. And little girls with strawberry blond hair who Lucas doted on and
catered to their every whim.

She needed to shake herself from the fantasies and understand her
place in his life. If she allowed herself to indulge in their truce, then once it
was over, the heartache she would endure would make the state of her sanity
unbearable. However, she couldn't convince her heart otherwise. What was
the harm in creating more memories to indulge in before she started the next
chapter in her life?

"What a perfect idea to enjoy a picnic today," Abigail gushed,
twirling around in a circle at the splendid scenery.

The trees were in full bloom, offering shade from the bright sun.
Wildflowers were taking their first peek from the winter chill. The birds
chattered away, singing a melody in the background.

Lucas offered her a sheepish expression. "I owed you a picnic from
the one I ruined last year."

Abigail beamed at him, not allowing those memories to ruin their day. "That you did, Lord Gray. But I have forgiven you."

Lucas stilled at how she addressed him, but her eyes were twinkling, and he realized she only teased him. He helped her spread the blanket out and offered her a hand to settle on the ground.

Abigail tugged the basket toward her. "What delights have you packed for our picnic?"

She pulled out the exact meal she had prepared last year. She had drawn Lucas's name for the picnic during the house party. While he had been engaged to Selina Pemberton at that time, it had never stopped Abigail from wishing differently. So when luck flipped to her side by drawing his name, she had prepared all his favorite foods. However, before they even ate, they had argued over her desire to gain employment. She had stomped off into the woods, only for Lucas to follow with his objections.

Then she had angered him more when she laughed over how Selina and Duncan's boat tipped over and drenched Selina. Duncan had mocked the lady, and Selina fired insults back at him. The pond water soaked Selina's dress, and the moss clung to the fabric, making the sight of the haughty lady entertaining amusement for the afternoon. At the time, she had only held a dislike for the lady, but now they shared a close friendship.

Lucas winked at her. "A few of my favorites."

"Well, at least we enjoy the same foods." She fixed them each a plate and rested her back against the tree.

"Did you notice we share many things in common?"

Abigail nibbled on a piece of cheese. "I suppose that is why we are excellent friends."

Lucas arched an eyebrow. "Are we not more than friends?"

He risked ruining her relaxed attitude by asking this question. But her silence about them kept him wondering if there was more to explore in their relationship.

Abigail arched her own eyebrow. "Are we?" She turned his question back to him. "That is a question best answered by you."

Lucas nodded at her meaning. He wished he had never asked because it caused her to lose her lighthearted mood and brilliant smile. Now she sat quietly, picking at her food and frowning.

"There is only one fault with our meal I apologize for, but Cook insisted on packing them." He opened a container full of cherry biscuits.

Abigail covered her mouth, but the laughter spilled out anyway. And once again, he restored the mood to an enjoyable atmosphere. Lucas popped the treat into his mouth and moaned at the delicious sensation of the biscuit melting on his tongue. Abigail shook her head at his silliness and grabbed one for herself. They spent the rest of the meal enjoying each other's company.

After they cleared away their luncheon, Lucas laid back on the blanket and closed his eyes. His belly was full, and the warm weather lulled him into taking a nap. He slept little during the night because every time he closed his eyes, he remembered their kiss and ached to share more with Abigail. Lucas fought against his tiredness, but exhaustion won over.

Abigail's gaze lingered on Lucas as he fell asleep. She hadn't meant to turn his question back on him, but her curiosity had won out. Was it so wrong of her to force Lucas to speak on where they stood? Abigail didn't think so. The kiss they shared spoke volumes. Now she only needed Lucas to speak the very words she longed for.

She reached over and brushed the hair from his eyes. "Lucas," she whispered. When he never stirred, she spoke the words she had longed to speak for what seemed an eternity. "I love you."

Even though he never heard her, her heart floated higher for confessing her true feelings. Her fingers slid along his cheek and across his lips. How she longed for him to draw her into his arms again and kiss her. She would forgive him for anything if he granted her a kiss each day. She was foolish for indulging in her fantasies, but their time together slipped away to where all she held was memories. Was she foolish to create memories out of her fantasies?

Abigail stretched out a considerable distance from Lucas. While she wished to lay her head on his shoulder and press her body against him, it was highly improper, especially in the light of day. For if anyone came upon them, Abigail's reputation would be ruined. A lady or not, the same standard consisted for every girl. Even now, them enjoying a picnic without a chaperone violated proper decorum.

But Colebourne allowed relaxed rules amongst his wards as long as they stayed within the guidelines of appropriate behavior. Abigail grew weary of maintaining the stricture she set forth for herself to never bring shame to her name. And all to showcase herself as a presentable bride for a certain marquess who refused to buck society. As much as Abigail wanted to resent Lucas, her heart refused to.

Abigail laid her head on her bent arm and stretched her hand out. Lucas lay with his palm open. She rested her fingers on his hand, allowing herself a brief touch. Her eyes slowly closed. She decided a small nap wouldn't hurt.

Lucas awoke with a start. An amazing dream starring Abigail gripped his senses. He dreamed of her plastered against him, professing her love while their lips and bodies entwined, making passionate love to one another. When a knee jammed into his side and an arm flung across his neck, his body stiffened, ready to attack.

However, when his attacker moaned in a breathless whisper, "Oh, Lucas," only one part of his body remained stiff.

His eyes drifted open to find Abigail sprawled across him. Her soft curves molded against him, inflaming his desires. Lucas bit back a moan when she started caressing his chest in her sleep. Her fingers trailed a path down and across his stomach and back up again before her hand curled around his neck. Abigail wiggled closer and sighed before settling back into her slumber.

The fingers on his nape set him on fire. The heat traveled through him, some areas more intensely hot than others. Abigail's breasts pressed against his side. He glanced down and noticed the dress had shifted during her nap. He only had to reach up and undo a single button, and her breasts would spill forth for his pleasure. Without Lucas realizing his intention, his hand rose and hovered over the temptation. The devil in him taunted him to slide the button through the hole, while his proper conscience pleaded the case of Abigail's virtue. Lucas slammed his eyes shut, clenching his hand into a fist before lowering it to his side.

When she shifted again, he opened his eyes to see if she awoke, but she hadn't. Instead, her dress tugged lower, exposing a nipple. Lucas moaned at the tempting berry teasing him to sample a taste. His need to act like a gentleman was slipping out of his control. He licked his lips, imagining how the sweet temptation would explode on his tongue.

His cock hardened to an unbearable ache. He needed to shift away without waking her before he acted on his desires. But the wondrous sensation of Abigail wrapped around him kept him still. He was capable of handling this like a gentleman. He started reciting multiplication tables in his head to distract himself. When that didn't work, he attempted to fool himself. Abigail was like a cousin to him, really. But that failed miserably.

As embarrassing as it would be for Abigail, he must wake her before he fulfilled every fantasy he held of them together.

First, he would start by bending his head and devouring her sweet nipples. Because after he sampled one, he would need to undo the rest of the buttons and sample the other. For a taste comparison, of course. Then he would ravish her lips as his hand slid up her dress and teased her legs to widen so he could caress her wetness. He would draw forth her pleasure until she screamed his name out across the open fields. His lips would capture her screams and draw them into his soul. Once she lay sated, then he would strip the gown from her body and build her desire again, leaving no part of her untouched. His lips would leave their own path of fire, setting her aflame.

Lucas brushed his hand across her chest. His fingers sank into her softness. Abigail moaned in her sleep, jerking him back to reality. What had he been about to do? He gulped. He had almost overstepped the bounds of suitable behavior. Ah, hell! Who did he fool? Their very intimate embrace had surpassed proper decorum.

He started with division tables, hoping the difficulty would cool his libido. Only this time, he argued with himself. He refused to subject Abigail to the same behavior his cousins had indulged in with their spouses before they spoke their vows. But he now understood why they had acted as they had. The only reason that kept him from fulfilling his desires was that he was unsure of his decision to make Abigail his bride. It wouldn't be fair of him to seduce her, no matter how tempting of a package she might be.

Abigail floated awake from the most amazing dream ever. She dreamed of Lucas wrapping her in his embrace and rousing her with the softest of caresses. She didn't want to awaken, so she kept her eyes closed, praying it was more than a dream. However, the longer she pretended to stay asleep, the more depressing reality became.

She felt a warm blush wash over her when she peeked one eye open to see she had sprawled across Lucas. His hand lay on his chest in a fist, and when she raised her gaze, she saw his eyes held tightly shut. His lips moved, but no sound came forth. Then he shook his head and started over again. However, this time, he mumbled out a group of numbers.

How was she to explain herself? After she fell asleep, she had managed to cover the distance separating them. And topping off her mortification, her hand clung to his neck. Her fingers itched to run through his hair and sink into his silky strands. Perhaps even encourage him to dip his head for a kiss. She would eagerly return his kiss with her own passion.

She kept staring at her hand, wishing it was her lips instead. She longed to kiss a trail down his neck and across his chest. Her eyes followed the path of her imagination, and she gulped at the sight of his chest. It was broad and well-formed and in need of her lips upon it. Abigail stilled at where her thoughts took her.

Lucas noticed the change in Abigail. She had awakened. He opened his eyes and lowered them to encounter her heavy-laden gaze. It was filled with desire, matching his own need. When her hand sank into his hair, every argument he held not to claim her lips flew away with the soft breeze surrounding them.

"Ah, hell," he muttered. He didn't hesitate to take her lips under his and devour them.

The mortification Abigail felt fled when his lips ravished hers in a soul-searching kiss. Each stroke of his tongue across hers led Abigail to abandon her morals. She only wished for his kiss to never end. Her body ached for his caress. As if he could read her thoughts, his arm circled her to bring her closer, and his other hand boldly caressed the top of her shoulder, down her arm, across her stomach, and up to her chest.

The cool air brushed across her breasts, and she realized she had exposed herself to Lucas. His thumb brushed across her nipple, tightening it into a hard bud. She pressed her breast into his palm, needing more of his wonderful touch. When his lips kissed a trail down her neck, Abigail silently begged for him to replace his fingers with his mouth.

Lucas paused. "I should not, but I cannot help myself."

He lowered his head and drew a bud between his lips. The sweet flavor of berries exploded in his mouth. His tongue circled the treat, drawing out purrs of delight from Abigail. Those sounds only intensified his need to suck on them for hours on end. He tore at the buttons holding her dress together and spread the material apart. He withdrew his arm around her and tugged on the strings to her chemise. Thankfully, she didn't wear a corset.

When he reached his treasure, he moaned from the sheer torture of her exquisite offerings. His hands molded to her breasts and lifted them to his lips. Moving from one sweet berry to the next, his tongue flicked across them, and he filled his appetite with her sugary sweetness. Abigail's hand drifted to his head, holding him to her chest while he pleasured the both of them.

"Lucas." Abigail's moan filled the air.

He must stop, but he had lost the hold on his resistance. Abigail writhing in his arms only pushed him to abandon every gentlemanly act he had remaining. He swept her dress above her knees and caressed her silky limbs. Lucas trailed his finger along the crease of her thighs, and she opened them willingly. He needed no other encouragement.

Abigail pressed into his hand. An ache consumed her, one only Lucas could help ease. His fingers glided into her wetness, searing her with his heat. She arched into him after he slid a finger inside her core. With each stroke in and out, Abigail unraveled further out of control. When he slid another finger inside and pressed his thumb to her wetness, Abigail whimpered her need.

"Lucas, please."

He answered her plea by drawing her nipple between his lips again and sucking on the bud as his fingers plunged in and out of her. "Fly, my little bird."

Abigail lost herself at his command. She felt herself hurtling off a cliff, only to float at the sound of Lucas's voice, encouraging her to be free.

Lucas pressed against Abigail's hip, seeking relief from the building pressure of his cock. While he stopped himself from taking her, he sought the comfort of her curves to ease the ache consuming him. He drew her into his embrace and pressed her head against his chest. With each ragged breath he drew in, he tried to quiet his body's demand. Abigail had softened under him but still clutched onto his shirt. Soft kisses landed on his chest once Abigail regained her senses.

Abigail couldn't help herself. She wanted to pleasure Lucas in return. His smooth chest was hard beneath her lips, and she wondered if the rest of him felt the same. Her fingers toyed with his button. She wanted to free them but worried he would think her behavior too scandalous. When he clenched her hands, she discovered her answer.

"Abigail, you must stop," Lucas clenched out between his teeth, fighting his desire. He wished for nothing more than to allow her to continue, but he had overstepped his bounds enough for today.

Shame washed over Abigail at her brazen attempt to undress Lucas. Obviously, he didn't want her touch. She tried to roll away, but he held her firm.

"You misunderstand."

Chapter Six

Abigail shook her head, too upset to speak. She tugged her hands out of his grasp and gathered her dress to cover herself. Lucas tried to help her, but she swatted his hands away. She scurried to her feet and hid behind the tree. Fighting back her tears, she lowered her dress down her legs and tied her chemise. With hands that shook, she finished buttoning her dress. Abigail pressed her head against the tree, drawing forth the strength to face Lucas she didn't think she possessed.

Lucas jumped to his feet, wanting to rush after Abigail to soothe her, but he gave her the privacy she needed. He paced back and forth, working up the courage to apologize for his ungentlemanly behavior, a behavior he had fought to indulge in but he was helpless when he held Abigail in his arms.

Abigail stepped from the tree and moved to the blanket, sweeping it up into her arms and holding it in front of her chest. She glanced at Lucas and saw the stricken expression across his face and knew he regretted his actions. She tried to hold back her despair, but a tortured moan escaped. He stepped forward to reassure her, but Abigail took off. She would fall to pieces at his feet if Lucas offered any sort of comfort.

"Abigail, wait," Lucas shouted at her departing form. When she didn't stop, he muttered, "Ah, hell."

He gathered the picnic basket and took off after her. He didn't need her to utter a word to realize she had misunderstood why he stopped her from unbuttoning his shirt. Her tortured expression and the tears in her eyes spoke of what she believed.

The sun started its descent, and the impending darkness increased his need to reach her before she entered the manor. He didn't want anyone to notice the state of her distress, nor the grass stains on her dress. Lucas took off at a run.

Abigail swiped at the tears streaming along her cheeks, but a fresh batch kept falling in their place. She heard Lucas behind and tried to run. However, the blanket got in her way and tripped her. She couldn't lose it or else she would have nothing to cover her disheveled appearance with. If any of the servants or Colebourne saw her, they would draw their own conclusions and she would bring shame upon herself.

She wrapped the blanket around her dress, finding it easier than carrying it. Also, it helped to increase her pace. She drew closer to the manor and realized she would be clear once she snuck through the door and escaped through the secret passageway.

However, luck wouldn't remain on her side. Lucas had reached her, swinging her around to face him. He clutched her arms, stilling her as she fought off his hold.

"Stay still," Lucas hissed, trying to catch his breath.

Abigail's eyes widened at his tone, and she didn't make another move. He didn't mean to frighten her but needed to explain why they had stopped before she disappeared into the house and stayed hidden until everyone arrived.

"Ahh, Abby." He wiped the tears on her cheeks away. He never wanted to hurt her, but at every turn, he made her miserable. Lucas now understood why she wanted to move away.

He wrapped his hands around her cheeks, brought her face closer, and placed a light kiss on her lips. She still didn't move, but he only had precious seconds before she erupted on him. Abigail was a sensitive creature who always cried first, then her temper would explode. All the signs pointed to her fury. Her eyes narrowed, she bit at her bottom lip to keep quiet, and her chest heaved with each breath.

"I will not apologize for my actions this afternoon. Because to apologize would show I regret every kiss and caress. Which I do not. Your gift this afternoon was only a sample of what I desire from you. I desire to kiss every inch of you while we make love. Because, you see, I am a greedy bastard and one afternoon with you in my arms will never satisfy my needs." He paused, noting how her breathing had calmed, but her glare continued to pierce him.

"I want you to prepare yourself, Abigail Cason, for I mean to pursue you until you are mine. No governess position or other gentleman my family members mean to dangle in front of you—nothing will stop me from possessing you, heart and soul."

Abigail poked him in the chest and gritted her teeth. "Then why, Lord Gray, did you stop me from touching you?"

A wicked smile spread across Lucas's face. "Because, my love, when you strip the clothes from my body, it will be in the privacy of my bedchamber and in front of a fire with a soft bed I can lay you upon as our souls become one."

Abigail gulped at the passion blazing from his eyes. Still, she must resist his charm. If not, then she would transform into a meek girl again, begging for any attention he would grant her. No matter how tantalizing his kisses were or how the stroke of his fingers lit her on fire, she must stay strong.

Abigail scoffed, regaining her power of resistance toward Lucas. "My love? Are you not taking your smooth words a little too far, my lord?" She brushed off his hold and rushed away. Once she reached the manor, she made the mistake of looking over her shoulder. When Lucas reached out to grab her, she dropped the blanket to block his path and hurried inside, hoping to escape anyone's notice, but she ran smack into Selina and Duncan.

"Steady now." Duncan grabbed Abigail before she fell flat on her face. He withdrew his hold after he steadied her. However, Selina wrapped Abigail in her arms, squeezing her in an affectionate hug.

"Now what is this nonsense about taking ourselves off to Charlie's?" Duncan asked Oakes.

"Well, that is . . ." Oakes floundered.

Abigail had never seen the butler at a loss for how to respond. Not to mention the guilty expression covering his face.

"How were you able to travel through?" Abigail interrupted.

"Abby!" Lucas called out from the doorway. He stumbled inside, juggling the picnic basket and blanket. He stopped in his tracks when he saw his cousin. "Duncan?"

Duncan bowed. "At your service, my lord."

Lucas scowled. He held no patience for his cousin's tomfoolery. "I suppose the road is clear. When are the other heathens expected to descend upon us?"

"Lord Gray, your comment is uncalled for!" Abigail reprimanded him.

Lucas arched a brow at Abigail's formality. "I do not believe it was, *Miss Cason.*"

Duncan glanced back and forth between Lucas and Abigail, noting the tension simmering between them. He also took in Abigail's disheveled appearance and his cousin's surly mood. If he wasn't mistaken, it would appear Lucas and Abigail had shared more than a picnic.

"The road to Colebourne Manor is perfectly fine. We traveled separately from my parents," Duncan explained.

"I hope your delay was not because of anything dire," Abigail said.

Duncan winked at Selina. "No, nothing too dire."

Selina turned red, and Abigail knew their delay was because of marital bliss. The thrill Abigail had felt when Selina married Duncan wasn't only because it freed Lucas from a betrothal agreement out of his control, but also because once Selina married Duncan, her true self shined through. No longer was she a spiteful shrew; instead she was a delight Abigail shared a close friendship with.

Selina beamed at her husband. "Nothing dire at all."

Abigail continued to stare at Duncan and Selina as they lost themselves in each other's gazes. The look they shared was one written in romantic stories. Abigail wished that for herself. She stole a glance at Lucas and saw him frowning at the lovely couple. She shook her head. He would never understand undying love. Lucas was hopeless, and Abigail needed to give up any notions that he would change.

This was only the start of the remaining week. Once everyone arrived, it would be couple after couple showing their devotion to the one they loved. Over and over. While she enjoyed watching their happiness, sometimes depression would set in, leaving Abigail with a vulnerability she didn't wish to endure.

"Did you say there was nothing wrong with the road?" Abigail asked.

"We traveled on it with no problems," Duncan replied.

"I do not understand," Abigail stated in confusion.

"Well, 'tis simple. Carriages and horses travel across the road to reach their destination," Duncan teased.

Selina lightly slapped Duncan on his arm. "Silence, husband. It appears if there is a slight confusion about our arrival."

"Oakes?" Lucas bellowed, stopping the butler's escape.

Oakes turned. "Yes, my lord?"

"Please explain," Lucas demanded.

Oakes cleared his throat. "'Tis best if the duke explained." Before Lucas asked him any more questions, the butler scampered away.

Duncan laughed. "You have frightened him."

"That conniving coot," Lucas growled.

Selina's eyes twinkled. "Is Colebourne playing matchmaker again?"

Lucas snarled. "He never stopped."

Abigail gasped at Lucas's sharp tone. "If you will excuse me." She rushed away, not waiting for a response.

Selina turned to Lucas, shaking her head in disappointment. "You have not changed one bit. Why she loves you is beyond me. But keep with your insensitive remarks and soon Abigail will come to her senses." She strode off after Abigail, wanting to offer her friend comfort from Lucas's foolish words.

Duncan slapped Lucas on the back. "When will you ever learn? Your father gave you the perfect opportunity to win Abigail's hand, and you keep blundering it."

Lucas raked his hands through his hair and strode off for his study. He didn't care if Duncan followed him or not. But he knew he would. They were as close as brothers, and Lucas always confided his troubles with him.

Even when Duncan stole his bride, Lucas had never allowed it to come between their friendship.

He poured himself a shot of whiskey and slugged it back. Then he repeated it twice more. Duncan yanked the bottle from his hand before he took another swallow and pointed at the chair. But Lucas defied him and paced back and forth in front of the fireplace instead.

Duncan took a seat and waited patiently for Lucas to gain control. Quite a few minutes passed and Lucas was in no better of a mood than when Duncan arrived. Since Lucas refused to discuss his problems, Duncan would have to drag them out of him.

"Do you want to discuss the picnic you shared with Abigail?"

Lucas stopped pacing and glared at Duncan. That subject was taboo and only between Abigail and him. "No," he growled.

Duncan nodded. "That is fair. Should we discuss your father's latest machinations?"

Lucas threw his hands in the air. "What is there to discuss? He is relentless in forcing Abigail and me together."

"So, your interaction with Abigail is still forced?"

"That is not what I meant."

"Then please explain," Duncan ordered.

Lucas slumped in a chair. "I don't know where to begin."

"Perhaps at the beginning," Duncan replied with sarcasm.

"Fine. Father said the storms wiped out the road. Then he has taken all his meals in his bedchamber, pleading he needed more rest."

Duncan frowned. "Is he sick again?"

Lucas shook his head. "No."

"Have you spent this time alone with Abigail?"

"Every available second. It was as if the past year never happened. We fell back into our comfortable friendship."

"So nothing untoward has occurred between you two? Because it appeared that Abigail might have spent the afternoon getting tousled."

Lucas growled. "Do not speak of Abigail in that regard."

Duncan nodded. "I apologize."

Lucas wiped his hand along his face. "I don't believe I am as strong as you," he confessed.

"You are. You only choose not to believe in the love you could share with Abigail. And until you do, you must break your ties with her. 'Tis not fair to string her along and give her false hope." Duncan sat forward. "You must see how you break her heart each time you speak in disgust at your father's matchmaking mischief. With each derogatory remark, you make her feel unworthy of your love. Then when you turn around and lay on the charm, she believes you have fallen in love with her. When you kiss her, it only shows proof of your devotion. You confuse her with your actions, and Abigail doesn't deserve this treatment."

Lucas stayed silent during Duncan's lecture. Every word he spoke held truth in them. But he refused to stay away from Abigail. It was too much for anybody to ask of him. Once the rest of his family arrived, Duncan and Selina would share his blunderings with them. Then he would receive a lecture from every single one of them.

"Do you agree?" Duncan asked.

Lucas stood. "No." He offered no more, leaving Duncan alone. He needed to find his father and demand for him to stop his matchmaking. It had gone on long enough. His father's attempts only impeded his own.

Well, that and his own foolish behavior.

Chapter Seven

Selina hurried up the steps, on her way to Abigail's room. Her friend's stricken expression at Lucas's cruel words upset Selina. She had noticed upon her arrival how Abigail had fallen victim to Lucas Gray's charm once again. Her letters the past few months had declared her intention to move forward with her life and stop waiting for Lucas to declare his love. Abigail had made plans to become a governess, and Selina feared those plans had changed.

When she reached Abigail's room, she found the maid pressing her ear against the door, muttering to herself.

"Polly?" Selina called out the maid's name.

Polly jumped, startled at getting caught eavesdropping. "Lady Forrester, I was only . . ."

"You are fine. How is Abigail?"

Polly wrung her hands together, glancing at the door. "In a terrible fit. I can hear her crying, then she goes off in a tyrant about arrogant, conceited lords who . . . I cannot repeat what the miss is saying. I never knew Miss Abigail held knowledge of such words."

Selina patted the maid's hands. "'Tis to be expected when one deals with Lucas Gray. Do not fret. I will calm Abigail."

Polly nodded, taking herself away. Selina sighed. Within a matter of minutes, every servant in the manor would learn of Abigail's tirade about Lucas. Polly was a dear, but she couldn't keep a secret.

Selina opened the door without knocking and strolled into the bedchamber as if it were her own. She found Abigail curled up on the divan, crying. Selina closed the door, rushed to her side, and drew her into an embrace. At one time, they had disliked each other, but now they were as close as sisters. Selina's heart ached at Abigail's despair. She hoped her husband was calling Lucas out for his poor behavior.

"Oh, dear. Everything will be well. I promise."

Abigail hiccupped. "You cannot make a promise against the impossible."

"Yes, I can," Selina stated with confidence. "After all, I will become a duchess one day and I deem it so."

Abigail laughed and wiped at her nose. "You don't even want to become a duchess anymore."

"But it is my destiny, and I have accepted it," Selina answered smugly.

Abigail smiled wistfully at her friend. "You will be the grandest duchess of the ton."

Selina shook her head. "Not standing next to you, my friend."

Abigail pinched her lips. "That day will never happen. As of this moment, I am finished with Lucas Gray. I have fallen out of love with him." Abigail rose off the divan and started pacing. Her temper rose with each step. "What I held for him was never love but a silly infatuation I am no longer indulging in."

Selina scoffed. "Bollocks."

Abigail blushed at the profanity. "Selina!"

Selina arched a brow. "Do not act Miss Innocent with me, Abigail Cason. Polly had her ear at your door and told me of the improper words you used to describe Lucas."

Abigail blushed. "Mmm."

"Mmm is right. If you are no longer in love with Lucas, then please explain the *grass stains* on your *wrinkled dress*."

"I tripped and fell," Abigail lied.

"Pshh, another lie."

Abigail refused to defend herself. Because no matter what she said, Selina would discover the truth. Abigail was a horrible liar. She could never perfectly tell a lie because, with any fib she ever uttered, guilt ate away at her.

"Then can you explain your plump lips? Because they appear as if someone kissed them quite thoroughly," Selina taunted. Abigail stayed silent, so Selina threw question after question at her about Lucas's kissing abilities. "Is Lucas a swell kisser? Did he make you weak in the knees? Does he make you want to throw all sensible behavior to the wind?"

"Why do you ask me questions you are quite aware of what the answers are? You shared a kiss with Lucas before and have firsthand knowledge of them," Abigail answered with exasperation.

Selina shook with revulsion. "You are aware of the reason behind our kiss. And it is a memory I have forgotten and wish never to relive. So my answer would be no to every single question. But I was not asking myself but you. So please tell."

Abigail sighed, throwing herself across the bed. "Yes. Yes. Yes."

"Finally. He took long enough. I feared you would become an old maid before he even made an attempt."

"Why are men so difficult?"

"Because they are stubborn fools."

Abigail rolled over and propped herself up with her elbows. "But Duncan wasn't. He knew he wanted you and he let nothing stand in his way of making you his."

"I wish I had a token of advice to help you," Selina said.

"Like I said, it does not matter anymore. I have accepted Lord Ross's offer. When we arrive in London, I will become a governess to his two daughters."

"Lord Ross?"

"Yes. He is the lord I wrote to you about. He learned of my interest in holding a governess position and wrote to me last year. But I had to decline his offer when Colebourne fell ill. But since then, his governess is leaving his employment because she is getting married. So he offered the position again. He has holdings in England and Scotland, so I will split my time between the two countries during my employment," Abigail explained.

"Have you learned anything else about this lord? Has Colebourne vetted his standing in society?" Selina asked with curiosity.

"Yes. They have corresponded and Colebourne gives his approval."

"Mmm. Interesting," Selina murmured.

"What is?"

"The name seems familiar, 'tis all. Now let us return to the kiss you shared."

"Kisses," Abigail muttered.

"Kisses?" Selina exclaimed.

Abigail nodded, turning bright red.

Selina clutched at her chest. "Oh my, the ever prim and proper Abigail Cason and the stuffy Lucas Gray shared scandalous kisses. I am shocked."

Abigail sat up, rolling her eyes. "Please. Our kisses were tame compared to every other courtship in this family. Well, the one we shared last night anyhow."

"And the kisses you shared today?"

"Have you ever felt like your heart exploded when you were kissed?"

A dreamy expression lit Selina's face. "With every kiss from Duncan."

"Ohhh."

"Can you walk away from the feelings Lucas ignites in your soul?" Selina asked.

"I must protect my heart. Every single marriage in this family has shown proof of how they have persevered through the obstacles thrown in their paths. Especially your marriage to Duncan. It has only made the bond each couple shares stronger. Still, Lucas overlooks it all, remaining stubborn," Abigail argued.

"Do you not owe it to your heart to try one last time?"

"It is pointless. Lucas doesn't share the same desire as I do."

Selina laughed. "Oh, you are as blind as he is. Lucas seduces you with his eyes wherever you roam. He is constantly seeking your company. Not to mention the longing he holds for you. That man wishes to strip you naked and make you his."

"Then why did he stop this afternoon?" A fiery blush warmed Abigail's cheeks.

Selina smiled knowingly. "Is that the reason for your unhappiness when you returned from your picnic?"

Abigail's hands fluttered in the air. "He . . . That is . . . You know."

Selina's eyebrows lifted. "No. I do not know."

Abigail's entire body grew warm at discussing how Lucas seduced her, only to reject her affections. How humiliating! "Lucas and I were intimate this afternoon. Then when I tried to return his affections, he jerked away and would not even allow me to touch him."

Selina nodded, understanding Abigail's dilemma. However, it wasn't as severe as she imagined it to be. While Lucas seduced Abigail, he also tried to protect her virtue.

Selina sat next to Abigail and gathered her hands in hers. "He pulled away because even though he seduced you as a scoundrel, he acted honorable."

Abigail frowned. "I do not understand."

"You, my friend, are a temptation Lucas is finding difficult to resist." Selina smirked.

"Pshh." Abigail scoffed. "I see you have adapted to your new family well. The Forresters can spin a fanciful tale on anything."

Selina laughed. "I shall take that as a compliment. Now how you proceed is entirely your choice."

"I have made my decision." Abigail remained stubborn.

Selina rose and walked to the door. She paused, turning slightly. "Might I offer a suggestion?"

"If not you, then I am sure once everyone arrives tomorrow they will not hesitate to offer their advice."

Selina smiled. "I am sure every single lady will offer the same suggestion."

"And that is?" Abigail asked with sarcasm.

"There is magic in the secret passageway. You only need to make your wish as you travel along the passage. And you will find your wish granted."

Selina didn't wait for Abigail to refute her idea. And Abigail held no convincing argument against it. She stared at the mirror that led to the secret passageway. Every single one of her friends had used the secret passage and their happily ever after wish came true. Was she bold enough to venture to Lucas's bedchamber? How would he react if she were to throw herself at him? Would he think her a wanton woman trying to trap him? Or would he accept her love?

If she were to take a chance, it must be this evening before everyone arrived tomorrow. Selina and Duncan would turn a blind eye, but her friends, nay her family, would force a union between Lucas and her. Abigail accepted the fact of never becoming Lady Gray. However, it didn't have to stop her from experiencing Lucas's love. She now understood why her friends had sacrificed their virtues for the gentlemen they loved.

Was she willing to make the same sacrifice without breaking her heart?

Chapter Eight

Lucas stripped off his waistcoat and cravat, dropping them in a pile by his wardrobe. He pulled it open, looking for an old shirt and trousers to change into. He decided a late-night ride might help calm his fury. Dinner had been a trying affair. The tension rippling off him had made it impossible for him to enjoy the meal.

He was furious with his father and wanted to declare his frustrations, but Selina had pleaded with him not to cause any more strife. His father had convinced the entire staff to lie to him and Abigail about the condition of the road. When, in fact, travelers continued to use the road with no problem. On his way to his father's room, Selina had confronted him, demanding what his intentions were concerning Abigail. He had been about to inform her to mind her own damn business when Duncan appeared, ready to defend his wife. Lucas had growled at their interference and took off to sulk.

During dinner, Abigail had ignored him once again but laughed joyously with his father, Duncan, and Selina. Duncan had tried to draw him into the conversation, but Lucas continued with his brooding. His father even had the gall to apologize to Abigail for his dishonesty. And she had accepted his apology gracefully, telling him she understood his reasons. Then she made him promise to stop with his matchmaking, and he agreed. Which was false. His father would never stop until he achieved his goal. Why was Abigail so naïve to believe otherwise?

Abigail.

She was a fiery temptress he ached for. He sat across from her at dinner, lost in a haze, because the images from this afternoon kept flashing before him. Every movement, every throaty laugh, every smile reminded him of how he had brought her pleasure and the sighs that had echoed around them. His need to hear those sighs again almost pushed him to steal into her bedchamber. But he had overstepped himself and ruined any chance he had when he offended her.

Lucas tugged off his boots and shucked his trousers. It would appear he had angered the servants again, since his valet never came to his room and during dinner they set his meal far away, making him reach for his plate. He should just travel to London on the morrow. Because once the rest of his family arrived, he wouldn't have a minute of peace.

"Lord Gray, I have made a decision." Abigail's soft whisper floated over to him.

He shook his head. Now madness had set in, because he imagined Abigail stood in his bedchamber, talking to him. Lucas swiped a hand along his face.

"Do you not wish to hear about my decision?"

Lucas stilled. He struggled to imagine hearing her voice again. He slowly turned and saw Abigail standing near the mirror. Lucas grabbed the quilt to draw around his middle. He stood in shock at her appearance but still drew her in.

She was his dream come true. Every fantasy he held, she turned into a reality. Her fiery hair hung down her shoulders, and she wore a simple white robe. Lucas wondered what lay beneath it and how quickly he could dissolve her of it. She stood before him acting boldly, but he noticed her trembling and the hesitation in her gaze. However, he was powerless to respond.

But he could show her a sign of encouragement. He walked toward her until they were but a breath apart. Lucas gave her a nod to proceed. If he opened his mouth, he feared the wrong words would spew forth and he would frighten her away. He may be foolish but not enough to ruin any chance she gifted him with this evening.

Lucas waited for Abigail to explain her reason for appearing in his room, looking like a package that needed to be unwrapped. When she untied her robe and let it fall at their feet, he stood dumbfounded. He was unsure how much time passed before he responded. Only when doubt filled her gaze and she bent to gather her robe did he react.

Abigail took a chance, and she had failed. At least she could say she had tried. Before she lost the rest of her dignity, she needed to leave. However, Lucas lifted her in his arms, kissing away every doubt she held. He never gave her a chance for the speech she prepared. Instead, he held her as a cherished treasure.

When she arrived, Lucas had been in the middle of undressing, oblivious to her. Instead of stating her presence, she had watched him strip every bit of clothing off. He was indeed a fine specimen. Lucas held the ability to make Abigail forget every ladylike thought she should have and turn her into a wanton temptress.

Lucas carried Abigail to his bed, not once taking his mouth from hers. Each kiss held desperation. He stretched above her, pressing intimately against her. She set his soul on fire. Every noble act he swore he wouldn't subject her to vanished when she bared herself to him. A gentleman only held the ability to restrain himself so much when temptation lay at his feet. And when the lady who held his heart gave him permission to love her, who was he to refuse?

"Abigail," Lucas moaned.

"Yes, Lord Gray," Abigail murmured.

Lucas scowled before he kissed her fiercely. "Lucas."

She slid her fingers into his hair, guiding him back to her lips. She whispered, "Lucas," before he devoured them again.

Each kiss stretched into another as their hands wandered, exploring each other. Their moans whispered around them. Lucas rolled them over and Abigail lay across his chest. Her breasts branded him. She shifted and her hardened nipples softly scraped across him.

He pulled back from their kiss and speared his hand through her hair. "I need to make love to you."

"We have all night."

"Forever," Lucas demanded.

Abigail didn't answer him because forever wasn't in her plans. She only wanted this one night. She was realistic enough to understand her place in Lucas's life. No matter how much everyone supported a union between them. Abigail understood Lucas better than anyone else. While his conscience would demand he marry Abigail for taking her virtue, it wouldn't be his first choice. He wanted a bride from an upstanding family of the ton. Not a bride whose mother had a child out of wedlock and never married.

Instead of agreeing with Lucas, she lowered her head and placed one soft kiss after another along his neck and across his chest. She hoped to distract him, and she did. When her hands slid down his stomach, he didn't stop her this time and helped guide her on how to please him. He pressed her palm against his hardness.

Abigail gasped at his strength. He dropped his hand, allowing her to explore on her own. Abigail wasn't a naïve lady. She had learned a lot from when the servants gossiped and when each of her married friends let intimate details of their marriages slip. Her hand wrapped around him and the silky smoothness glided in her grasp. She peeked a glance at Lucas to find his lids lowered as he watched her pleasure him.

When she tightened her grip and brushed her thumb across the tip, he swore his pleasure. A dew of wetness slid across her thumb. She lifted it to her lip and sucked the taste of Lucas onto her tongue. When she licked her lips and moaned her pleasure, he flipped her over onto her stomach.

"You temptress minx. You aim to torture me with your seduction." Lucas pressed into her back, whispering in her ear. "But not before you suffer from my seduction first."

Abigail shivered in anticipation as Lucas's mouth trailed a searing path down the middle of her back. His hand slid underneath to cup her breast. While he started his torture, his fingers pinched her nipple, bringing forth an ache she needed relief from. However, Lucas had only just begun. How he turned her seduction around on her, she'd never know. Nor did she care as long as he never stopped.

She was heaven and hell in his arms. The answer to his prayers, yet a promise out of his reach. Every silken inch of her begged for his touch, and he wouldn't deny the passion they could share.

His hand slid lower, sinking into her curls. Wetness coated his fingers at the first stroke. Abigail whimpered and pressed her buttocks up against him.

"It appears my minx is impatient," Lucas teased.

His fingers teased her too, brushing across her wetness, then pulling away. Each time, she pressed against his cock. He didn't know who he tortured more. His lips trailed down her back and over her buttocks.

Abigail moaned her need. "Lucas, please."

"I aim to please you, my love," Lucas promised.

And he did with each soft stroke of his tongue. Abigail parted her thighs for him and he raised her hips to savor her sweetness. Each drop of her dewy wetness coated his tongue, and he drank from her with a thirst only she could fulfill. His finger slipped in and out while he kissed her thoroughly. She pressed her core into his mouth, searching for her release. Lucas strung Abigail's need toward a higher power. Every time she gave, he took greedily, wanting her to give more of herself over to him.

Abigail's legs shook around him when she exploded. Lucas stroked her thighs as she floated back to him. He rolled her over, needing to see her reaction. A flush spread across her cheeks and traveled along her chest at his bold stare. Her breasts rose with each deep breath she drew. Her unfocused gaze held the look of a woman well satisfied. A smug smile settled over his face until a single tear leaked from Abigail's eye.

His satisfaction crashed to a halt. It was then that he realized there was no turning back for them. Abigail was his world. He refused to live another day without her by his side.

"I am sorry." An apology escaped from him.

Abigail stared into his eyes, searching for answers. But he didn't think she found what she searched for. "I'm not and it saddens me that you are."

"Then why are you crying?"

"Because your love was so beautiful."

"Oh." Lucas was speechless and unsure how else to respond.

Abigail watched confusion cloud Lucas's gaze. He held himself stiffly above her, uncertain how to act. His apology was only a reaction to her tears. When, in fact, his hardness pressed into her, making its intention known. A man sorry for his actions wouldn't remain so close with his interest so obvious.

A wicked smile spread across Abigail's face. "Lord Gray, you are not finished yet, are you?"

Lucas growled.

Abigail wrapped her hand around Lucas's cock. "Lucas." Her need echoed in her whisper.

Lucas lost what remained of his honor when she smiled like a temptress and teased him with her touch. "No, I am not."

He slowly slid inside her, drawing out their pleasure. Abigail tried pressing up, but Lucas held her hips still. "Patience, Miss Cason."

He slid in deeper and paused. Waiting.

"Yes, Abigail," he moaned as he slid out and back in again. "Abigail, Abigail, Abigail," he chanted as he slid in and out.

Abigail wrapped her arms and legs around Lucas, clinging to him. Her body moved in sync with his. Each time he pulled out, she pressed into him, not wanting their bodies to part from one another. Nothing else compared to the heights he took her to as he worshipped her. Their bodies danced as one, each movement drawing out their passion to the sweetest melody.

Lucas had never experienced this intense passion with another soul. He had longed for this connection for years, even though it was his fault for denying them happiness. He was a fool who finally understood the madness of love.

Lucas grabbed Abigail's leg and raised it up to his hip, pressing deeper into her. Her nipples rasped across his chest, begging for him to kiss them. His head lowered, drawing a bud into his mouth. He sucked the berry like a man feasting on the most succulent of fruits. Abigail's fingers scraped along his back, her body begging him to meet her demands. He'd never get enough of her.

Abigail tightened around his cock with short pulses that built into longer ones. He raised his head and stared into her love-filled eyes. He watched her unravel around him, spreading her wings to fly. But he refused to have her fly without him. He drew her lips in a kiss and pressed in harder until he soared with her.

Lucas drew Abigail across his chest, clutching her to him. He never wanted her out of his arms again. She was the other half of his soul. It was foolish to think he could ever live without her. The demand for them to wed was on the tip of his tongue. But if he did, he would sound like a brute and he had behaved in that manner more than once of late. No. Abigail deserved a grand gesture when he declared his love.

Abigail luxuriated in Lucas sliding his hand up and down her back in a soft caress. She was barely holding it together. She wanted to burst into tears from their exquisite lovemaking. It was beautiful beyond words. She sensed Lucas was already making plans for their future. He would feel an obligation now since he had ruined her. Abigail wished to be more than an obligation. Ever since her mother died so tragically, she had been an obligation to the Duke of Colebourne. She didn't regret giving herself to Lucas, but she refused to become a burden.

With much reluctance, she slipped from his arms and wrapped the bedsheet around herself.

Lucas grabbed the sheet, stopping Abigail from leaving his bed. "And where do you think you are going, my bewitching minx?"

Abigail tugged the sheet higher. "I must return to my room."

Lucas pulled her back into his arms. "You are going nowhere. I have not gotten my fill of you yet."

The kiss Lucas gave Abigail had her melting in his arms again. With each pull of his lips, Abigail's need to return to her room became forgotten.

His tongue slid inside to stroke hers. They danced until the flame consumed them.

"I do not think I ever will," he whispered in between kisses.

Abigail clung to Lucas at his declaration. She never wanted to relinquish her hold. She had promised herself an evening with Lucas, and the evening was far from finished.

Dawn hovered on the horizon when Abigail inched out of Lucas's bed. He had fallen asleep after teaching her the many delights of lovemaking. She had watched him sleep, storing away the memories until the sky lightened.

Her gaze lingered on Lucas as she drew on her robe. She took a step toward the bed but stopped herself. She almost brushed the hair from his eyes. However, she wouldn't stop after the first touch, and she couldn't risk being discovered by anyone.

She eased the mirror open and snuck back inside her bedchamber. Abigail heard the first signs of the servants starting their day. With a heavy sigh, she donned her nightgown and crawled into bed. There were a few hours left to sleep before everyone arrived, and she needed her rest before the chaos began.

But how was she to sleep alone when she only wanted Lucas's arms holding her?

Chapter Nine

Gray stretched as he came awake and searched for Abigail, only to find the spot next to him empty. He blew out a breath at his foolish notion of Abigail sleeping in his bed. He rubbed at his chest from the ache of her absence. The only simple solution to his dilemma was to find Abigail. He wanted to share his plans of stealing away to Gretna Green with her.

If they traveled to Scotland, they would avoid all the fuss of a proper marriage ceremony. Also, he would beat his father at his own game. No. His father wouldn't take victory with this match.

Gray strolled along the hallway to Abigail's bedroom when his cousins descended on him.

"Where might you be off to?" Charlie smirked.

"I plan on escorting Abigail to breakfast," Gray explained.

"'Tis not necessary. We are having our breakfast ritual in Abigail's bedroom this morning," Evelyn said.

Jacqueline pinched her lips. "Your behavior is most improper. Knocking on Abigail's door without a chaperone nearby. Tsk, tsk, what will Uncle Theo say?"

"What are your intentions with our Abigail?" Gemma asked.

Gray gritted his teeth, drawing in what remained of his patience with his interfering cousins. "Why have you arrived so godforsaken early? You were not due to arrive until luncheon."

"And such language, too. For shame. And to think only this morning Aunt Susanna called you a gentleman," Jacqueline scolded.

Selina walked up behind them. "Lucas? A gentleman? Mmm, not lately, ladies."

The other ladies turned toward her in astonishment. "You do not say?" Charlie inquired.

Selina waggled her eyebrows. "I do. Perhaps we should ask Abigail for the details of how wicked Lord Gray has been in our absence," Selina teased.

Gemma slid her arm inside Selina's. "Yes, let us."

Evelyn and Jacqueline paired up to follow, and Charlie patted Lucas's cheek on her way past him. They invaded Abigail's room, leaving him alone in the hallway. When he left his bedchamber, he had felt lighthearted, ready to conquer the world. Now he worried his cousins might ruin his chances with Abigail. Especially if they learned he had ruined Abigail last night.

He returned to his bedroom to change his clothes. He decided to take the ride he had planned before Abigail came to him. Gray wasn't in the mood to join everyone else for breakfast. His father and uncle would banter back and forth while Aunt Susanna kept the peace. If he showed his face, he would find it difficult to stay quiet about his plans. He needed Abigail's permission before he shouted it to the universe.

Gray saddled his own horse because the stable master, Emory, was directing the stable boys where to store the many carriages and horses for the duration of their stay. He led his stallion out of the stable, where he met Duncan and his cousins' husbands. They each stood wearing a smirk at his predicament. He glared at Duncan for confessing his secrets, and Duncan only shrugged his indifference. It would appear his cousin sought revenge for Gray kissing Selina before they spoke their wedding vows. Even though Selina had asked for a kiss, he remained the guilty party.

"There he is, gentlemen. Or should I address us as scoundrels?" Kincaid asked sarcastically.

It was only fair for his friend to taunt him since Lucas had expressed his anger with Kincaid for seducing Jacqueline. And now he did not differ from the gentlemen standing before him. He had fallen to their level of seducing an innocent lady.

"I know Selina loves when I am addressed as such," Forrester quipped.

Everyone groaned and hid their smiles because their wives felt the same way.

"Now, we should give Gray here a chance to explain himself before we defend Abigail's honor," Sinclair replied.

"Do we need to defend Abigail's honor?" Ralston growled. "Gemma is nearing the end of her pregnancy and must remain calm."

Gray swung onto his horse and looked at Worthington. "Do you want to offer your piece?"

Worthington shook his head. "I believe your own guilt is working against you."

Gray nodded and rode away before they continued with their insults.

"Shall we join him?" Worthington asked.

"Yes," Forrester answered.

Each gentleman readied their horses and rode off after Gray. They caught up with him near the pond where he lay under the tree with a hat covering his face. He expected them to follow because they didn't differ much from their wives. They would offer their advice whether or not he wanted to hear it.

"It took you long enough," Gray drawled.

"How would that reflect on our friendship if we allowed you to handle this on your own?" Kincaid quipped.

"Do I have a choice?"

Each gentleman answered with their own negative remark, leaving Gray frowning at their disapproval.

"Every single one of you either ruined one of my cousins or my fiancée." He scowled at Duncan. "Yet you hold an opinion on how I have treated Abigail."

"Only because your behavior toward Abigail this past year has been atrocious. You are lucky none of us has called you out for it," Sinclair declared.

"We grow weary of our wives' complaints against you. Please, show mercy on us," Ralston pleaded.

Gray jumped to his feet and paced back and forth. "What would you have me do?"

"Either confess your undying love or set her free? She deserves no less," Forrester ordered.

"I planned to, but everyone arrived early and now your wives have her surrounded. Who very well might convince her to stay away from me."

Worthington threw his hands up at this friend's foolishness. "Why would they convince her otherwise? They all wish for you to marry Abigail. How are you still so dense?"

Gray frowned. "They appeared upset with me when I attempted to escort Abigail to breakfast."

Sinclair quirked an eyebrow at him. "And when have your cousins not made your life difficult?"

He was a fool. A fool of the highest order. Perhaps he should discuss his plan with his friends. They would inform him if it was the wrong choice.

"I want to convince Abigail to steal away with me to Gretna Green," Gray admitted.

"Absolutely not!" Worthington growled.

"Why not?" Gray asked.

"Trust me. You will regret it. If I could change my courtship with Evelyn and give her the wedding ceremony of her dreams, I would," Worthington answered.

Gray advanced on Worthington. "Courtship? Is that how you describe seducing my cousin while you imagined you were with her sister instead?"

Sinclair stepped between them. "Gentlemen, let us focus on one scandalous courtship at a time."

"Your plan is rubbish, cousin," Forrester declared.

"It is perfect, and I have changed my mind. I will no longer discuss my relationship with Abigail with any of you. If I want your advice, I will ask. Which in case I never will. So mind your own business and inform your busybody wives to do the same," Lucas ordered.

Ralston had stayed quiet for most of the discussion. He wasn't as familiar with Gray as the other gentlemen were. They all held a long friendship with him, and he had only become better acquainted with Gray through his marriage to Gemma. But he needed to offer a bit of advice. If he didn't, then Gemma would never forgive him, for she loved Abigail like a sister and hated to watch her friend's heartache.

"We only ask for you to tread carefully with Abigail. If you love her at all, then you must show her how much you cherish her. She has lived in doubt for so long, she expects nothing else. You must set your pride aside and declare your intentions with honesty. Not hide in fear of how others will perceive Abigail. If not, then I think I speak for every gentleman present when I say if you hurt Abigail, we will defend her honor." Ralston finished his speech, and each gentleman stood next to him in support.

Gray stared at his friends and noticed how none of them wavered to his side. None of them understood the pressure on his shoulders to make a successful choice for a bride. Who were they to threaten him? He had stated his intention to marry Abigail. Why couldn't any of them offer their support?

Their opinion didn't matter. He would convince Abigail of his plans and show everyone how only Abigail's wishes mattered.

Even if his conscience silently whispered how mistaken he was.

Chapter Ten

Abigail finished serving the hot chocolate and pastries before sitting next to Gemma on the divan. Her friend struggled to hold the plate with her swollen belly getting in the way.

"Should you have made the trip to Colebourne Manor?" Abigail asked.

Gemma rubbed her stomach. "You sound like Barrett. He is a mother hen, hovering over me constantly."

"Perhaps because you are due to give birth any day now," Charlie drawled.

Gemma waved her statement away. "Nonsense. I have a month left, and Barrett's carriage is fit for a queen. I am no more ready to give birth than Jacqueline."

Jacqueline smirked. "I have two months before my baby makes its arrival."

Evelyn took a sip from her cup. "Either way, neither of you should have traveled. We were scheduled to arrive in London in a week."

"Now tell them the real reason you risked the visit," Selina chastened her.

Gemma gave Abby an impish smile. "I wanted to be here for the success of Uncle Theo's last match."

Abby frowned. "There will be no match between Lucas and me."

Selina coughed behind her hand, muttering, "Bollocks."

Charlie laughed. "I see with your marriage to Duncan you have acquired a more colorful vocabulary."

Selina waggled her eyebrows. "Among other skills."

"Yes. I can see where you would," Charlie replied.

"Ladies, let us focus on Abigail," Jacqueline reprimanded them.

Gemma glanced back and forth between Abigail and Selina. Abigail glared at Selina while Selina's face held a secret she was dying to reveal. When Selina arched her brow at Abigail's glare, Abigail's cheeks turned a charming shade of pink. Their exchange stoked Gemma's curiosity to learn what had happened between Abigail and Lucas. If Abigail's blush was any sign, they had shared more than a kiss.

Gemma bombarded Abigail with questions. "He finally kissed you! How was it? Was it everything you imagined it to be?"

Abigail brushed away some imaginary crumbs off her lap. "No, he did not," she denied.

"Bollocks!" Charlie looked over at Selina. "It is most exciting to declare, is it not?"

Selina nodded. "Yes!"

"If you two do not behave, we must ask you to leave," Jaqueline scolded them.

Selina and Charlie tried to hold in their amusement but failed. They broke out into another round of giggles. It was hard to believe they had once been mortal enemies, always striking out with revenge whenever their paths crossed. Now they contributed in calling out Abigail in her denials. She might as well confess before Selina told her own version of the story.

"I confess. Lucas kissed me yesterday while we took a picnic. But nothing else happened."

"Abigail?" Selina warned.

Abigail tried to look innocent. "What?"

"How do you explain your grass-stained skirts, disheveled hair, and lips that looked beyond ravished if you shared only a kiss?" Selina asked.

"The same way her hair and lips look this morning?" Charlie tilted her head.

Selina nodded. "Exactly."

Abigail blew out a breath, realizing her assumptions stood correct. Selina would blab of all her indiscretions if she didn't confess herself. "Fine."

"By Selina's description, can we assume our cousin has overstepped his gentlemanly manners and seduced you?" Evelyn asked.

"Perhaps I seduced him," Abigail confessed.

"Oh, my!" Gemma gushed.

"Now you must spill the truth of what took place while everyone stayed at my residence. Did Uncle Theo's plan work?" Charlie inquired.

Abigail narrowed her gaze. "What plan?"

"The one where Lucas finally came to his senses and made you his," Charlie answered.

"I will never be his. But if you inquire whether we enjoyed each other's company, then the answer is yes."

"Finally," Gemma replied.

"No, 'tis not what it seems. Lucas and I will not wed. I am taking the governess position with Lord Ross once we arrive in London. Nothing is any different today than it was yesterday. I do not hold the quality of a duchess for Lucas. I hold no proper standing in society and I never will. The same argument stands. He will never profess his love and I refuse to offer mine. We shared one night together, and that is all we will ever share. No more."

"But . . ." Gemma started.

"But nothing. I have come to terms with our relationship. Now I insist everyone in this family come to the same terms. Lucas is meant for a lady of the highest standings, and I am meant for a life of servitude," Abigail declared.

"You do not believe that," Gemma argued, shaking her head. "You are more valuable than what you give yourself credit for. Your last name may not be Holbrooke, but you are as much a Holbrooke as we are. And anyone who says otherwise can go hang."

Abigail didn't answer. She grew weary of the same argument. For the past year, she had shared the same conversation multiple times with everyone in this room. And each conversation had ended in the same regard, with them urging her to remain hopeful. Well, Abigail had given up all hope and accepted her position in society for what it was. She loved this family dearly, but they must also accept how others viewed her and how she would never find acceptance outside of this small circle.

"Do you hold belief your only value is one of a servant?" Evelyn asked in disbelief.

"Yes," Abigail answered.

"There is no way we can change your mind?" Jacqueline inquired, and Abigail shook her head. Jacqueline offered Abigail a wistful smile. "Then as your sisters, we accept your determination and offer our full support."

The other ladies voiced their objections, but Jacqueline gave them each a disapproving stare. The entire room grew quiet. They each drank their hot chocolate and ate their pastries. Each of them stared at Abigail, hoping to coax her into changing her mind.

Finally, Jacqueline took pity on her. "Tell us about your position in Lord Ross's household. I thought he found another governess since you couldn't join him at his estate after the holidays."

"I will be a governess to his two young daughters. They sound like the sweetest souls from his letters. Lord Ross dotes on his daughters and fills the letters full of praises for their accomplishments. The governess he hired fell in love with a shopkeeper and is getting married. Once he found out, he wrote to me and offered the position again," Abigail explained.

"How did Lord Ross learn of your desire to become a governess?" Evelyn asked.

"I posted an advertisement in the *London Times* last spring when we stayed in London."

"The entire time you led us to believe you gave the season a chance, but you were secretly plotting your escape." Gemma's tone reflected how Abigail's actions had hurt her.

Abigail winced, for that was exactly what she had done. None of them understood how those functions placed her in awkward situations. If the ladies of the ton didn't meet her with snide remarks, then the gentlemen made up for her distress with their scandalous suggestions. She never whispered a word of the many propositions made by them. It would have angered her family and caused her more embarrassment once Colebourne released his wrath. After the season ended, she had realized how the ton would never accept her. Even if Lucas declared his love, she could never have him suffer from the isolation their marriage would incur.

"Yes."

"Why?" Gemma started crying, startling everyone.

Abigail tried to comfort her, drawing her hands in hers. Gemma was the closest person she had to a sister. Abigail's mother had served as a maid to Gemma's mother. They had grown up together and shared everything.

When they lost their parents, they had clung to each other to grieve. Abigail had found joy when her friend found her happily ever after with Barrett Ralston. Soon Gemma would become a mother and their lives would travel different paths. Throughout their friendship, Gemma had never understood how different their lives were and she never would.

"Because I watched every one of you find love and I realized I had no future with the one I loved. Even when his journey took a different path once Selina married Duncan." Abigail smiled over at Selina. "He would never accept me for who I am. I don't want a life where my own husband holds shame toward me. All of you must understand. Please, I beg of you."

"While we will never understand, we will accept your need to find happiness," Evelyn assured Abigail.

"You will?"

Gemma nodded, tears coursing along her cheeks. "I blame the baby for the tears."

Abigail drew Gemma into a hug. "I promise I will always be available when anyone needs my help. It is a stipulation I made with Lord Ross when I agreed to accept his offer."

"Will you at least have Uncle Theo meet with Lord Ross before you start your employment?" Charlie asked. "I cannot shake the strange sense I have about your position. It would relieve my worries if we had more details about Lord Ross since none of us have heard of him before."

"Colebourne has already corresponded with Lord Ross and has given his approval," Abigail informed them.

"He has? What is his opinion of the earl?" Selina asked with skepticism.

"He thinks I have made an excellent choice for an employer."

Selina rose suddenly. "Please excuse me, ladies. I forgot I must tell Mama some news from the village before I forget again." Selina rushed out of the bedchamber before anyone questioned her further.

Abigail smiled after Selina. "I am thrilled Selina has found such joy with Duncan. She is a different lady from when we first met her."

"Yes, she is. We all underestimated her," Charlie agreed.

Gemma wiped the tears from her face. "Will you tell us about your new charges?"

Abigail smiled at her friends' acceptance. She enlightened them with the earl's letters and even mentioned how she felt a kindred spirit with the widower. Even though they stayed silent about Lucas, they wouldn't remain quiet for long. Before they departed for London, they would each attempt to change her mind. Whether individually or as a group remained to be determined.

Either way, Abigail would stand firm in her decision. No matter how much it broke her heart.

Chapter Eleven

Selina strolled into Colebourne's study without knocking. She wanted to catch the conniving matchmakers unguarded. They were whispering and stopped their discussion when she came upon them. Colebourne sat back with a smirk, and Papa broke out into a huge smile at her appearance.

Mama stood up to wrap her in a hug. "I am happy to see you and Duncan made a safe arrival. When you did not follow our carriage, I grew worried."

When Selina blushed, Ramsay laughed. "I told ye they were still playing at newlyweds."

Selina arched an eyebrow. "Playing?"

Ramsay chuckled. "Exactly."

Colebourne laughed with them. "I see you have not grown timid with this ancient relic. You give as good as he dishes out."

Selina nodded. "I must. If not, then he is relentless in his taunts."

Colebourne smiled. "Shall I offer you my sympathy, my dear?"

"No need. It is a welcoming joy to belong in a comforting family."

"Did you need something?" Mama asked.

Selina held her arm out to the chair. "May I?"

Colebourne rose and helped her to sit down. "Is there something on your mind you wish to discuss?"

Selina smoothed out her skirt and placed an innocent smile on her face before she accused them of their latest scheme. "I underestimated the lengths you two will go to achieve success in your match between Abigail and Lucas. I am most impressed."

Theo and Susanna exchanged glances of confusion. Their only attempt had been the delay of everyone's arrival. Theo shrugged and gave a slight nod to Susanna to not give away their confusion. Susanna winked and turned her charming smile back to Selina.

"Yes, well, all is fair in love and we must prevail in uniting the lovely couple since they remain stubborn in admitting their love," Susanna remarked.

"I can only say bravo to this plan of yours," Selina complimented her.

Colebourne tried to use guilt to secure Selina's trust in the little mystery she had brought to their attention. "Since you learned of our deceit and ruined my plans to give Abigail and Lucas time alone by your early arrival, I hope you can keep our little secret to yourself."

Selina bit her bottom lip, deciding if she should keep their secret. "I am unsure."

"Leave the poor girl alone. She has only recently become friends with the other lasses," Ramsay argued.

Theo scowled at his brother-in-law for interfering. "Don't you need to visit with Cook to sweet-talk her into baking your favorite pastries?"

Ramsay narrowed his gaze right back at Colebourne. "And leave Selina alone with you scheming matchmakers? No. I need to protect my son's wife. Also, there is no need because Cook is already baking my favorites as we speak."

Susanna patted Ramsay's hand. "Now, dear, we only want to know how much Selina has learned of our devious attempt and to plead our case."

Ramsay kissed Susanna's cheek. "Nonetheless, I shall remain. Because now I am curious to learn what you have plotted."

Colebourne hmphed. "Nosy Scotsman."

"Meddling Sassenach," Ramsay muttered.

Selina giggled. "Oh, I have missed your squabbling."

Colebourne frowned. "I haven't."

"Me neither," Ramsay added.

"Another time, boys," Susanna reprimanded them but smiled fondly. "Now, Selina, how did you figure out our scheme?"

Selina gave them both a scolding stare. "Lord Ross?"

"The earl who has offered Abigail a position in his household?" Susanna asked.

"The very one." Selina smirked.

"What about him? I vetted him, and if Abigail accepts his offer, he promised to allow her plenty of visits with our family. If she decides to leave us, then I approve of Lord Ross's home," Colebourne answered.

"Of course you would, considering Lord Ross does not exist. Oh, he exists, but he hasn't used that title for years. Not to mention, his daughters are grown ladies and only one has survived," Selina offered with a bittersweet smile.

"What is this nonsense?" Colebourne scowled. "Who is behind playing Abigail false? I will ruin the reprobate."

Colebourne's temper rose with Selina's accusation. He had placed his trust in the earl on Abigail's welfare, only to learn of his insincerity. How was he so gullible to believe the gentleman's words?

"Calm down, Theodore," Susanna murmured. She shot Ramsay a panicked look. Theo had grown red, and the scowl on his face displayed how his temper was on the rise.

"You can stop with your pretending, Uncle Theo. I know you and Mama used Granddad's title to play out your little scheme. However, when

Abigail discovers your game, you will end up bruising her heart, and we might never see her again."

Ramsay let out a deep chuckle. However, his laughter grew uncontrollable and tears soon leaked from his eyes. "Lord Ross. You two are craftier than I thought. I never even connected the name. Brilliant of you to recognize the title, lass."

"I learned every proper title Duncan will hold when he inherits. I cannot prepare our offspring if I am clueless," Selina explained.

"Lord Ross," Colebourne muttered, his eyes widening once he made the connection.

"Father's lesser title," Susanna whispered.

"Still playing innocent?" Selina asked.

Colebourne turned his charming smile on Selina. "A matchmaker must never give away his secrets. Especially if he wishes to make a successful match."

Selina rose once she realized they would never confide in her. "Please reconsider your actions. Abigail has suffered enough heartache to last a lifetime."

Susanna nodded. "We will take your advice to heart. Please stay silent until we decide on our next course of action. We promise it will not be for much longer."

Selina inclined her head. "I will give you until we leave for London. If you haven't confessed by then, I will inform Abigail and plead for her forgiveness."

After Selina left, a heavy silence filled the study. They stared at each other, with the impact of Selina's words all around them. If they weren't the ones who had corresponded with Abigail, then who was? How were they blind not to have recognized the title and the similarities shared between Abigail's Lord Ross and the real Lord Ross? Lord Ross was none other than Susanna's father. It was an old, forgotten title he never used.

Colebourne sighed. "Why didn't I recognize the similarities?"

Susanna shook her head. "I missed them too. Abigail wrote to me about the children. Their names are the middle names of Olivia and me. How did we not see this?"

"Because ye both are too busy plotting schemes to throw them together. But it seems as if someone else will claim victory with the match," Ramsay teased.

"Who?" Colebourne and Susanna asked.

"The boy," Ramsay stated.

"Lucas?" Susanna couldn't believe what her husband was suggesting.

Ramsay nodded. "The very one."

Colebourne shook his head in denial. "Nonsense."

"He is wooing the lass," Ramsay explained.

"Nonsense," Colebourne repeated.

Ramsay raised an eyebrow. "Then how do you explain his reasoning?"

Susanna frowned. "I fear he is prolonging Abigail's leaving by staging a false position for her. He refuses to marry her but also refuses to allow her to live her own life. Lucas believes he knows what is best for Abigail."

She rose from the settee and started pacing back and forth across the room. Each gentleman watched her, worried that Lucas's actions had set off her temper. Susanna was a mild-mannered lady who always showed grace even when her temper was in a snit. She had raised the girls to always brush aside their anger. However, after living with a high-strung Scotsman for the past thirty years, she had acquired a few traits to make any man quiver in fright if they angered her.

Susanna stopped behind a chair with a pinched expression. Theo had pressed his luck with many of his hairbrained schemes over the past year to make matches for his nieces. Each one had been more scandalous than the last. Yet he came out victorious with their marriages.

However, his son played a dangerous game with sweet Abigail. If they didn't correct it, it would have insurmountable consequences and affect every member of this family. Abigail was as much one of theirs as Lucas was. But if she discovered the enormity of Lucas's deceit, then she would leave them forever, as Selina stated.

"We must interfere," Susanna claimed.

Colebourne nodded. "I agree."

"How will ye fix this mess?" Ramsay quipped. "The boy already started his demise. I think ye should make him stew a bit."

Colebourne quirked an eyebrow. "Any suggestions?"

"Yea." Ramsay wore a devious smile.

"What is it?" Susanna barked, impatient with her husband.

Ramsay chuckled at her spark of temper. A few kisses should do the trick of calming the lass. He winked at her and Susanna only shook her head at him in exasperation, but her lips lifted in a smile.

"Invite Lord Ross to visit. Inform the children this evening at dinner how you need to rest longer and plan to extend your return to London by another week. Then inform Abigail while everyone is listening that you sent Lord Ross an invitation for him and his children to visit. Explain how you wish for them to meet Abigail's family before she starts her employment. Force Lucas to come to his senses before it is too late."

"Brilliant as always, my love," Susanna gushed.

Colebourne's lips twisted into a smile. "The plan is acceptable enough to earn you your stay."

"Pshh. Earn my stay. I gave you a way to make your boy squirm. That alone earns me more pastries."

The three of them laughed over Ramsay's comment.

Their plan sounded simple enough, but it would take the madness of love to succeed.

Chapter Twelve

Lucas trudged down the staircase. He had attempted to find Abigail throughout the day, but at every opportunity, one of his cousins ran interference. He wasn't even lucky enough to catch her eye. She avoided him. He didn't expect this reaction from her after the evening they spent in each other's arms. Lucas thought Abigail would find enjoyment in their pending union. He wanted to discuss his plan with her. Now he must wait until after the evening's entertainments concluded to steal her away.

He missed her. Not just her company, but Abigail herself. Over the past few days, he had felt the familiar kinship they shared. Now it had disappeared again, all because of his meddling family. His cousins' husbands regarded him with pity or else they taunted him with their opinions. And to think two of them were his best mates. Duncan shook his head in disappointment at him whenever their paths crossed.

He also had to deal with his cousins' reactions. They no longer tried to pressure him into confessing his love for Abigail. Every time he tried to approach Abigail, they informed him he was too late. What did they mean by that? His Uncle Ramsay would burst out into laughter when their paths crossed. Aunt Susanna and his father's pinched expressions stated how they weren't pleased with him at all.

He wondered how this evening's dinner would play out. He had hoped to convince Aunt Susanna to sit him next to Abigail, but getting his aunt alone to make his request was impossible. If his family wasn't offering their displeasure at his behavior, they avoided him.

When he strolled into the drawing room, his family grew silent. Each of them regarded him like an uninvited guest. Even Abigail slid behind Gemma's and Jacqueline's increasing figures to hide from him. He should just travel into the village and eat dinner at the tavern. At least there, no one would judge him.

"Ah, now that my son has joined us, we may dine," Colebourne declared.

"Gentlemen, please escort your wives into dinner," Susanna directed.

Lucas stepped forward to escort Abigail, but his aunt stopped him in her next direction after she hooked her arm through Ramsay's.

"Colebourne, be a dear and escort our lovely Abigail into dinner."

Colebourne bowed before Abigail and held out his hand. "My lady, shall we?"

Abigail smiled. "We shall."

Lucas scowled in displeasure. He watched each couple walk toward the dining room while he trailed behind them. Abigail glanced over her shoulder at him. He attempted a smile, but Abigail quickly looked away. His shoulders slumped at her rejection. Would he even be able to draw her away later?

When he came upon the table, he expected his aunt to sit him in between his cousins. However, she surprised him by placing him between Abigail and Charlie. Lucas was confident in his ability to handle one cousin. It was when the lot of them conspired together that he never stood a chance. Hopefully, if he kept Abigail entertained, it would limit any discussion with

Charlie, who, out of all his cousins, never kept her opinions to herself. She was more than happy to express her thoughts on any subject.

As they waited for the footman to serve the first course on their plates, Lucas turned to Abigail. He gazed at her, taking in her beauty. She wore her hair down with bejeweled combs holding her curls in place. The long auburn tresses trailed along her back. He groaned silently, remembering how he ran his hands through her curls as he made love to her. She looked beautiful with her hair spread out across the pillows. He ached to gaze at the sight again.

Abigail smiled across the table at Gemma and Ralston. Lucas wished for her to bestow her smile on him. He attempted to win one. "You look lovely this evening, Abigail."

"Is she not lovely every moment of every day?" Charlie interrupted.

"I think she is," Jacqueline added.

"No other rose holds the beauty of the one before us," Evelyn quoted from a poem she had read.

"A beauty like no other. Do you not agree, Duncan?" Selina asked.

"I agree, my love." Duncan winked at Abigail.

"Are you going to answer Charlie?" Gemma asked Lucas.

Lucas gritted his teeth. "Yes, she does."

Charlie shook her head, not pleased with the tone of his answer. "You do not sound very convincing."

His cousins planned to make his life difficult. For every punch, every degrading comment he made at their husbands, and his attempt at fleeing his marriage to Selina, all of it would come back to haunt him. They would make him suffer while seeking their revenge.

"Thank you, Lucas," Abigail whispered, shooting the ladies across the table a pointed glare.

She hoped they would stay quiet and not draw any unwanted attention her way. If the duke learned of her intimacy with Lucas, he would demand for them to marry. While she had always longed to become Lucas's bride, it was never under the duress of a forced marriage. Nevertheless, her heart understood how her wishes would never become reality because of her station in life. Now she stood on the verge of her plans coming to naught because of her friends' attempts to defend her.

She refused to make eye contact with Lucas in fear of what his gaze might hold. If it held regret, it would pierce her soul. But if his eyes held longing, she didn't know how she would react. Poor Lucas. Either way, she must not allow him to win. He was damned if he did and damned if he didn't.

Abigail listened to the flow of conversation floating around the table and a sense of melancholy settled over her. She would miss these family dinners where lively discussions filled the air with humor, debates, and the caring of a united family. Even though she shared no blood with this family, they had embraced her as one of their own from the very beginning. They each held a special place in her heart.

"Say the word and I will take care of him for you," Duncan whispered dramatically to her left.

Abigail turned and smiled. "There is no need. He has done no wrong."

Duncan winked. "This time?"

Abigail laughed. "This time."

Lucas growled at the laughter Abigail shared with his cousin when she wouldn't even grant him a simple smile. Charlie's snicker didn't ease his frustration any.

"Mind your own business, Charlotte," Lucas warned.

"And if I do not? You forget I am a married lady and I do not fear your threats any longer."

"I am sure I can uncover something you've done to inform Sinclair that he would not care for. Perhaps how you tried to ride the wild stallion that Father bought last week," Lucas threatened.

Charlie smirked. "Like I said, your threats are meaningless. Did you believe I wouldn't seek my revenge for how you treated Abigail during the season last year? Consider yourself warned, cousin. I've yet to share with the others what you said to her. Would you like me to share how you told Abigail she did not belong at those entertainments because of her standing in society?"

Lucas shrugged his indifference. He wouldn't allow Charlie to understand how much he needed her to keep her silence. If she informed the other ladies, then they would stop his pursuit of Abigail. "Gossip away."

Charlie frowned when Lucas didn't take her bait. "Perhaps I should just inform Uncle Theo how you ruined Abigail."

Lucas curled his fingers into fists underneath the table, holding in his fury. "I know for a fact you would never hurt Abigail by sharing that bit of news."

Charlie sighed. "No. You are correct." She paused. "However, I must warn you. If you so much as hurt Abigail anymore, I will not hesitate to seek my revenge."

"Warning noted."

Lucas turned away from Charlie, deciding to ignore her for the rest of the meal, then fixed his attention on Abigail. She sat quietly, not joining in with the conversation, a lovely smile gracing her face. He unfolded his fists and swiped them along his pants. He was as nervous as a young pup asking a girl for a dance. However, Abigail was skittish, and he feared scaring her off before he made his offer. Any wrong move and his entire family would explode with their wrath.

He brushed the tips of his fingers across her hand. She jerked her hand away but not before a sigh whispered past her lips. If the soft hush was any sign, it proved his touch affected her greatly.

"Abigail." He whispered her name so as not to draw attention to them.

The touch of his fingers singed her. She felt the slow burn spreading throughout her and ached to have his hands glide along her body. Sitting next to Lucas was the sweetest torture.

"Abigail," Lucas whispered again.

Darn. She had to answer him before anyone overheard. "Yes."

"Will you please give me your attention?" Lucas begged. Abigail turned her head slightly. "Please raise your gaze. I want to stare into your eyes and get lost in your soul."

Abigail gasped at his bold declaration, and her eyes flew up to meet his. The longing in his gaze left her speechless. It was one she was unprepared for and never expected. His gaze held a promise he meant to fulfill, one that would leave her with no doubt to the depths of his love. She shook her head to clear it, imagining his stare to be something it wasn't. But when she focused back on Lucas, his gaze only grew bolder.

A blush spread across Abigail's cheeks, turning them a lovely shade of red. "Yes. You look lovely this evening." He paid her the same compliment again. Which only turned her cheeks brighter.

"Hush," Abigail whispered.

"I will not. I have waited all day to speak with you. Why have you avoided me?"

Abigail glanced around the table, hoping for someone to come to her rescue. But every single one of them was a traitor. When she met their stares, they looked away and started a conversation with another dinner companion. She thought they were on her side, but obviously, she was mistaken. Her eyes narrowed as it raked the entire table. They were all in cahoots with Colebourne. Knowing each of them as she did, it was a contest to see who would make the match between her and Lucas.

Well, they would all lose. Even Colebourne himself.

"I thought it was the wisest course of action, considering how nothing has changed. I did not want to lead you to believe I expected anything from you," Abigail explained.

"What if I wanted you to expect something from me? Would you have considered paying me an audience?" Lucas asked with sarcasm, upset by Abigail's indifference.

Abigail sighed. "We agreed. One night and one night only."

Lucas growled. "No, you agreed. I promised nothing of the sort. I wish to make another promise to you. Will you become my . . ."

Abigail's eyes grew wide in panic. Lucas didn't mean to propose, did he? He couldn't. It would never do. Her eyes searched the table again for anyone to interrupt them. When her gaze fell on Ramsay, he was the only one to take pity on her. He gave her a nod of understanding.

"Abigail, I learned of your new position in Lord Ross's household. Colebourne told me of how he is a fellow Scotsman. I am afraid his name is unfamiliar to me. What parts does he hail from?"

"North of Inverness. He has a small holding he inherited from his grandfather."

Ramsay nodded. "Are you looking forward to caring for the youngins?"

Abigail smiled. "Yes. They sound most charming. He has two adorable daughters who get into all sorts of mischief. I cannot wait to meet them."

"How would you feel about meeting them sooner?" Colebourne asked.

Abigail pondered his question with confusion. "But I will meet him once we travel to London."

"I am afraid I must prolong our departure another week due to my health," Colebourne explained. The table erupted with concern over the duke's welfare, but the duke hushed them. "Nothing too troublesome. Susanna convinced me to take a longer rest and to enjoy my family before the rush of the season. So, I extended an offer to Lord Ross and his daughters to visit for a few days."

"That is a very generous offer," Abigail answered.

"One done out of selfishness, my dear. This way, his visit will put aside the rest of my concerns for your welfare. It would show how honorable the earl is, and it allows him to meet your family. Plus, it will be a joy to have young children around. Worthington's sister, Maggie, brought the house alive again with her youthful enthusiasm on her visit. I yearn for more enjoyment."

"Meddling old fool," Lucas mumbled.

Abigail stiffened at Lucas's comment. How can a gentleman gush lovely words one minute, then turn into a grumpy fellow who slandered his father the next?

Abigail glared at Lucas before offering Colebourne a charming smile. "Thank you. Your kindness and generosity are plentiful. I appreciate your gesture. Do you think he will accept your offer?"

"I wrote a letter this afternoon and sent it off to London via a footman. Hopefully, he will reply soon. And if he refuses, perhaps you should reconsider the position. Because if he is not willing to meet your family, then it leaves one to wonder if he will honor the requests we made."

Abigail nodded. "You make an excellent point."

"I am excited to meet your Lord Ross. He sounds most delightful," Aunt Susanna said.

"He is not Abigail's Lord Ross," Lucas growled.

Susanna waved her hand at Lucas's pettiness. "But isn't he?"

Lucas tightened his grip on the wineglass. "No."

Susanna smiled at her nephew with patience at his show of temper. "If you say so, dear." Then she turned and started talking with Kincaid about the new business he had started, ignoring how she had riled Lucas's temper.

Lucas threw his napkin on the plate and rose from the table. He had had enough of the insufferable dinner. The only reason he had joined them was for the chance to talk to Abigail, but he kept getting interrupted. He had been about to propose when Ramsay had to mention Lord Ross. A gentleman he had never met was a thorn in his side, one he would need to yank before he ruined any chance he had left with Abigail.

"Please excuse me, I have some correspondence I must finish. Welcome home, cousins. I hope we can visit and enjoy each other's company in the days to come."

He didn't wait for a reply. Lucas hid outside the door to listen to the comments made about him. However, he was sorely disappointed because no one mentioned him leaving early. Instead, he had to listen to them question Abigail about Lord Ross and his daughters. He closed his eyes, banging the back of his head against the wall at his foolishness.

Abigail's voice softened when she regaled them with Lord Ross's letters. Lucas listened to the praise at the earl's fatherly skills and the respect she held for him as a gentleman. Had she fallen for the earl and his charming words? It made him wonder every time she uttered Lord Ross's name.

Who knew one could hold jealousy of a fictional gentleman?

Chapter Thirteen

Abigail trailed behind Selina and Duncan. He had his arm wrapped around Selina's waist, holding her close. Abigail held no envy for them, only happiness for the love they shared.

Duncan pulled Selina off to the side, and Abigail heard him whisper to Selina, "I will join you soon. I only want to check on Lucas. He left in a temper, and I worry over his state of mind."

Selina stood on her tiptoes. "Another reason why I love you."

He drew her in for a deeper kiss, then winked at Abigail before he pulled away and sauntered off in the opposite direction. Abigail chuckled at the dazed expression on Selina's face as her husband walked away.

"How did I get so lucky?" Selina asked in awe.

"Because you deserve it," Abigail answered, drawing her arm through Selina's.

Selina smiled. "As do you. Perhaps we should follow Duncan. I will cover for you if anyone questions your whereabouts. From what I noticed, Lucas tried to get your attention during dinner."

Abigail glanced over her shoulder to see if anyone stood nearby, then pulled Selina around the corner for privacy. "I believe he attempted to propose to me before Ramsay interrupted."

Selina's eyes widened. "Oh, my goodness."

"Exactly."

"How would you have answered?"

Abigail frowned. "No."

Selina's eyes twinkled. "Your answer does not sound very convincing."

Abigail leaned against the wall. "I am so confused. He barely grazed his hand across mine, and I wanted to lean in and kiss him."

Selina giggled. "That would have shocked the table. Though it would also have been quite entertaining."

Abigail smiled at the vision. "Too scandalous?"

"Oh, yes, most definitely."

Abigail straightened. "Will you give my excuses? I am going to retire early this evening."

Selina nodded. "One day you must stop running."

Abigail attempted a smile. "But not today."

"Good night, my friend."

Selina watched Abigail retreat to her bedchamber. She understood the need to steal away some precious time from the Holbrooke family. While she had learned to love them, sometimes they were a bit too much. Although they meant well with Abigail, they also wanted to force her happiness, something Abigail and Lucas needed to discover on the path of their own making, not one directed by others.

Selina wanted to offer her support of Lucas along with Duncan. Her husband had shared with her the plans Lucas had for Abigail. While she didn't agree with them, she wanted to help him understand how wrong his decisions were. Selina paused outside of Lucas's study. The door stood ajar, and she was about to stroll in when Duncan's comment stopped her.

"Lord Ross? You fool!"

"I know. Stop calling me that. I have called myself that more times than I can count for the past hour."

Selina peeked inside the room. Lucas was slumped in a chair, drinking whiskey straight from the bottle.

Her husband paced back and forth relentlessly, running his hands through his hair. "You must confess," Duncan ordered.

"How? She will run off forever."

"What I do not understand is how your father hasn't pieced together your duplicity?"

"He is too preoccupied with his own schemes to pay any attention to mine."

"Are you mad?" Duncan asked.

"As mad as the rest of you." Lucas took a long swig.

Duncan grabbed the bottle from Lucas and took his own drink. "Why?"

Lucas threw back his head and stared at the ceiling. "At the beginning, it was to discover how serious she was about leaving. Once I discovered her determination, we had settled into sharing a weekly correspondence with one another. Then out of obligation, I offered Abigail a position."

Duncan shot Lucas a bewildered look. "A position for your two fictional daughters?"

Lucas winced. "I see the error of my antics."

"No! I do not believe you do," Duncan replied with sarcasm.

Selina struggled to understand what Lucas was admitting to. Lucas was the mysterious Lord Ross, not Uncle Theo and her mother-in-law? Selina closed her eyes at the enormity of the situation she had caused by accusing them earlier of this deception. Not only were they not the culprits, but she had also given them the ammunition to blow Lucas's identity to shreds. Now they had devised a new plan in their matchmaking attempt.

However, none of them understood the devastation this would bring to Abigail.

Abigail wanted to strike out on her own in search of happiness. And now it would all come crumbling around her with everyone's deception. Somehow Selina had found herself in the middle of it. Perhaps there was a solution to the situation.

Selina pushed open the door, striding inside. "Then help me understand why you started the correspondence back again when she wasn't able to take your offer after the holidays."

Duncan stepped toward her. "Selina, I swear I had no clue."

Selina held up her hand to quiet him and faced Lucas, waiting for an explanation. "Explain yourself," she ordered.

Lucas sat up straighter in his chair at her tone. He glanced at Duncan to gain any interference, but his cousin only shook his head, informing him he was on his own. During their betrothal, Selina had been a defying force, but she had softened after her marriage to Duncan. However, she stood before them now in all the glory every lady of the ton feared.

He gulped. "I missed her."

Selina looked at him with exasperation. "You missed her? You saw her every day."

"'Tis not the same."

Selina threw her hands up in the air. "Now I am more confused than ever."

Duncan guided Selina over to the settee and settled her next to him. "Why do we not let Lucas explain his mishap to us while we listen to him with a smidge of support? I am positive after he explains we will understand his intention toward Abigail."

Selina crossed her arms over her chest. "I am listening."

Lucas cleared his throat, stalling for time. His mind scrambled to explain the reasons for his foolishness. But his only answer was the one he had stated. "I missed her."

Selina sighed at the heartache reflected in Lucas's declaration. "You already stated so." Taking pity on him, she tried to coax out his reasoning. "How was it not the same?"

"She refused to talk to me for days on end. As she observed each courtship in this family, she grew more forlorn, and whenever I spoke to her, she misunderstood my intentions."

Selina quirked a brow. "Perhaps because you made her feel as if she was not your equal."

Lucas scowled. "No more so than you."

Duncan growled. "Leave my wife's previous behavior out of your drama. She has apologized and redeemed herself with Abigail. You will not tarnish their friendship by making Selina suffer remorse for her past actions, when you are the only one who continues to treat Abigail wrongly."

"My apologies."

Selina nodded her acceptance. "Why did you start the correspondence again?"

"I missed the connection we held from those letters. It was as if my father's mad matchmaking never happened and we were friends once again. Only through her letters, Abigail introduced another side of herself that she never showed me before and I in return expressed my true self to her."

"I understand. But why did you offer her employment again?" Selina asked.

Lucas sighed. "I panicked. She stated how she had another offer and explained how inappropriate our correspondences were. Abigail planned to accept the offer and didn't want her new employer to speculate on our friendship. So, I concocted a story of how my current governess had gotten engaged."

Duncan scoffed. "You have fabricated the entire ordeal. Hell! You used our own grandfather's name."

"And both your mothers' names," Selina added.

"What?" Duncan exclaimed.

"Tell him the names of your two little girls, *Lord Ross*."

Lucas winced. "Anna and Rose."

Duncan groaned. "You have sunken to a new low, cousin."

"It is romantic," Selina gushed. "Did you fall in love with Abigail while corresponding?"

Lucas swallowed hard. "I have always loved Abigail. Even when you and I were engaged, I longed for her. It pierced my heart to watch her suffer. Now her heart will become destroyed once she learns how I impersonated Lord Ross."

"You must confess before she learns the truth on her own," Selina urged Lucas.

Lucas sat forward. "How? Either way, I am doomed."

"But if you—"

"No," he cut off Selina with his firm answer.

"You can—" Selina tried again.

"Selina," Lucas warned.

"You have to try to . . ."

Lucas shook his head. "I will handle this on my own."

"How?" Selina asked, her irritation shown in that one word.

"I will pen her a letter stating how I have taken a bride. I will explain how my new wife has taken to the girls and she will care for them.

The letter will arrive tomorrow before the fiasco my father has planned comes upon us. I will let Abigail down gently."

"And your father?" Duncan asked.

Lucas's eyes narrowed. "I will take care of my father. Somehow, he figured out my deception and aims to unveil it to Abigail by forcing me to confront my feelings. I am confused about how he figured out Lord Ross was a fictional lord."

Selina sighed. "'Tis my fault. I might have accused them this morning of deceiving Abigail. I thought they were behind the mysterious Lord Ross. They convinced me they were and promised to end their deceit. Of course, I held belief in them. They are quite devious."

"You are not to blame. I should never have allowed it to reach these lengths," Lucas assured her.

Lucas walked to the window and stared outside. He had made such a grave error by impersonating Lord Ross. Now Abigail would suffer disappointment from losing her position, and he was to blame. If he thought he would have trouble convincing her to marry him before, then once she learned she had nowhere to run, she would only refuse him all the more. She would believe he only offered for her out of pity.

But not if he offered for her before the letter arrived from Lord Ross.

He must sneak into her bedchamber once the rest of the house retired. Perhaps he could convince her to ride away to Gretna Green before everyone awakened.

Lucas stiffened when Selina touched his arm. "What can I do to help?"

He turned and offered her a smile. "Nothing. I blundered our own engagement and it would appear that I am blundering my courtship with Abigail. While I thank you for your support, I cannot ask you to betray your friendship with Abigail. It is too precious and one that should have formed years ago. I did you a great injustice during our betrothal, and I will no longer allow you to sacrifice your happiness for me. Our arrangement ended the day you wed Duncan."

"Pshh. Nonsense. We are family and family always stands by each other's side. No matter the dilemma. I will stay silent for now, but understand this, I will praise the few attributes you possess to Abigail," Selina added with a wink before she joined Duncan at the door.

Duncan nodded his own support and swept his wife away. Lucas watched them leave with envy. While he had never loved Selina or suffered any heartache when she passed him over for his cousin, he missed the security his betrothal to her brought. When he thought he was set to marry Selina, he suppressed the love he held for Abigail. He accepted the terms of how they would never experience their own happily ever after. But when Selina married Duncan and ripped away his future, the ripples of the aftermath had affected him greatly. He'd fought with his emotions, trying to keep them at bay. But he had failed miserably.

Now he was forced to wed Abigail. It was the proper thing to do since he had ruined her. He did not differ from his cousins' husbands, after all. However, once they married, he would hurt Abigail by forcing her to endure the cruelty of the ton's judgment. They would never accept her, and every one of his peers would see her as easy prey. Abigail's happiness would wither away with each day of their marriage. And it would be all his fault.

Lucas decided to retire to his bedchamber. No need to ponder over what he must accomplish. He had a proposal he must make tonight. While he would be over the moon if she said yes, he also dreaded the word. Either way, Abigail would become his bride.

~~~~~~

Little did Lucas realize his father had overheard the entire conversation with Selina and Duncan. His son was under the impression that a simple letter withdrawing an offer of employment would solve his problem. But what Lucas didn't understand was the severity of how Abigail would react. He only hoped Lucas didn't blunder his explanation. Perhaps a visit from the boy's grandfather would help him come to his senses.

After all, his father-in-law was a formidable presence who would demand the truth.

Chapter Fourteen

Lucas stretched out his legs, shifting on the battered chair. The spring poking through the threadbare cushion dug into his back. At first light, he wanted to order a servant to dispose of the obnoxious piece of furniture. But he wouldn't because it was one of the few pieces Abigail had left of her mother. His father had rescued the chair when he learned of how the servants discarded Abigail's mother's belongings after she passed away. It was a comforting piece Abigail sought solace with when she suffered through her loneliness. The chair and a few other trinkets were her only reminders of a time she shared with her mother. He had never realized the piece stood on the verge of falling into shambles. He had never seen it before, but Gemma had described the value of it to him.

Gemma told him how Abigail used to curl up in her mother's lap every night before bed, and her mother would read her a story. After the story, her mother would sing Abigail to sleep. Lucas wondered if Abigail's mother's voice had been as beautiful as her daughter was when she sang. Did she express her emotions in the same haunting melody as Abigail did? He held a deep sense of regret, for he would never learn the answers to his questions.

Lucas focused his gaze on Abigail while she slept. When he snuck into her bedchamber, she had been fast asleep. He didn't have the heart to wake her, even though his body demanded otherwise. He kept fighting with himself not to crawl between the covers and join her. He wanted to wrap her in his arms and let her warmth invade his soul. Awaken her with tender kisses and listen to the sweet melody of her sighs as his hands stroked her awake.

When he first settled in the chair, he thought he had awakened her. She stirred, kicking off the quilt. When she never uttered a word, he realized she still slept. So he covered her, only to have her repeat the act multiple times. To say Abigail was a restless sleeper was an understatement. She thrashed around on the mattress as if she were caught in a nightmare. Only she never cried out once. Instead, she snuggled against the assortment of pillows surrounding her with a sigh.

He had hoped one of the restless episodes would startle her awake. But he grew disappointed the longer the evening lengthened. Lucas yawned. His lack of sleep settled over him, and he allowed his eyes to close for a second. He would wait a bit longer, and if she didn't awaken, he would return to his room, then come back in the morning and catch Abigail before she had her breakfast with the ladies. After that, they could make their announcement to his family together.

He yawned again before his head drifted down. His last thought before he fell asleep was a promise to awake before dawn.

However . . .

~~~~~~

Abigail awoke to her body trembling. She wrapped the sheet around her tighter, reaching out for the quilt to provide more warmth. However, her hand came up empty. She dragged her eyes open. As she searched the bed, she noticed the blanket had slipped to the floor. Abigail rolled over to hang off the bed, reaching out to snag the blanket. However, she caught sight of a pair of boots attached to a set of legs stretched out in front of her favorite chair.

Her gaze didn't need to travel higher to know who they belonged to. The goose bumps prickling her skin weren't from the chill in the air but from the awareness of Lucas in her bedchamber. She wished nothing more than to grab the blanket, roll over, and cover herself to hide from him. However, her body betrayed her by demanding she take in his presence.

Abigail's gaze slowly drifted higher, taking in the splendid view along the way. Her body grew warm as she admired Lucas in his relaxed state. His muscular thighs filled out his trousers, leaving little to the imagination. Her gaze swept across his arousal and traveled higher, only to return to take another peek. The gods had gifted Lucas when they created him. The evening before, she had experienced the strength of his arousal in her palm. She had even sampled a taste of his essence, but not enough to fulfill her hunger.

She kicked off the blanket when the heat of desire lit her body on fire. Abigail longed to satisfy the cravings of her every fantasy. Especially the one where she struck out with her wanton acts of rendering Lucas speechless. She moaned as she imagined the taste of Lucas on her tongue.

Abigail had turned into a depraved soul with no remorse for her sinful thoughts. However, in her defense, she was powerless to resist the passion shared between them since he first kissed her. She had waited a lifetime for his kiss, and she refused to deny herself the pleasure any longer.

With reluctance, she forced her gaze to continue its journey. His hands folded across his stomach, relaxed in sleep. Deep, even breaths raised his chest up and down. Lucas's head lay in an awkward position, leaning off to the side. He looked so peaceful, and Abigail hated to wake him, but she knew she mustn't allow him to remain in her bedchamber. It wasn't fair to lead him to believe they would share anything more, even though she longed for him to join her on the bed. She had promised herself one night only.

However, she made excuses about her decision when she fought the need to brush aside the lock of hair hanging over his eyes. Was she making a mistake by accepting the governess position with Lord Ross? After their evening together, did she stand a chance at winning Lucas's heart? If she gave him another night, would he admit to his love? Or did she only wish for the impossible?

Abigail's thoughts remained conflicted. However, they shouldn't keep her from making memories to keep her warm when she left Lucas. Abigail drew in her courage for the brazen act she was about to commit. His appearance in her bedchamber was the only encouragement she needed. Why else would he visit her room, if not to share in their desires? She wasn't naïve enough to believe a marriage proposal would ever cross his lips. No. He came to discuss Lord Ross's visit. She needed to distract him before he started off on another tangent.

Abigail slid off the mattress and crawled between Lucas's thighs. Her hands glided up his legs as she settled in closer. Her fingers sank into his muscular thighs as she remembered the pleasure of them pressing into her when Lucas claimed her. The buttons on the placket of his trousers released with ease. Abigail's hand dipped inside and withdrew the object of her desire. Her eyes grew heavy as her hand glided over the steely hardness. Her tongue darted out to wet her lips. Abigail's desires grew in anticipation of Lucas trembling in her mouth.

Lucas released the moan he held back while keeping a hold of his fierce determination of willpower. However, Abigail had taken over his control with the softest of touches he no longer wanted to resist. He fought to resist her and halt her before she went any further. But he crumbled when he saw the fierce passion clouding her eyes. A passion he needed more than his next breath of air.

At that moment, every doubt and argument he held with himself withered away. How didn't he understand the depth of the love he held for this woman before now?

Abigail bent her head, drawing him inside her mouth as her hair brushed across his thighs. The soft tendrils teased him with each swish. His hands sank into her curls, guiding her deeper in his pleasure. He threw back his head and moaned his gratification over her decadent gift. When her tongue swirled around his cock, teasing him, his stare fastened at the exquisite sight.

Abigail's mouth sank lower on his cock, her tongue stroking his desire to an unbearable ache. His fingers tightened on her luxurious mane when she stroked across the tip. When her mouth milked the tip, savoring his juices, he almost flooded her throat with his desire, but he latched onto what remained of his control. He refused to come like an inexperienced schoolboy. No. He was a selfish bastard who enjoyed the sight before him too much to finish. Abigail on her knees, unselfishly giving him the most exquisite pleasure a woman could give a man. A sight forever engrained into his memories.

Lucas's hands tightened in her hair, displaying how he tried to rein in his control. Abigail teased a trail of licks down the length of his hardened steel, eagerly waiting for him to fall apart under her act of love. Her tongue rose back up to the tip, circling slowly, drawing in each drop of his desire onto her tongue. She raised her eyes, and Lucas captured her in his gaze. His lids dropped heavy with desire, but his stare declared the passion she wrapped him in. However, he had yet to tremble the way she desired.

She wanted to undo him, to watch him succumb to the madness of their love. But wanting Lucas to fall victim to her charms showed how selfish her motives were. She wanted him to ache as he had never ached before. Abigail wanted to be a reminder of what he chose to resist. She wanted his undying love and devotion.

She held so many wants. When in reality, what she wanted most of all was the reality itself. Instead, she would grasp for what she desired most of all.

Lucas.

She pulled away and drew her teeth over her bottom lip, biting down. She stayed still. Waiting. She saw the desire building in his gaze, and the power of watching him unravel heightened her senses. His hands unloosened in her hair, only to tighten again as he fought for control. The pulse of his desire beat in her hand as she stroked him faster. Her thumb brushed his wetness down his length.

Lucas's breathing grew erratic as he waited for her to continue. She teased him on purpose. Why? He held no reason. He only knew how he ached for her to wrap her luscious lips around his cock and finish the madness she had started.

"Abigail," he growled.

A wicked smile spread across her face at his frustration. It spread wider when he trembled under her caress. His thighs shook with his need, tightening their hold around her. His fingers twitched as he guided her back to his cock. Abigail's mouth widened, closing over his cock with the sweep of her lips. Before she could tease him, Lucas's hips rose from the chair and he plunged deeper inside. The power of Lucas losing control invaded her soul.

As he lost himself with each stroke, Abigail's tongue pleasured him. The trembles she ached to experience surrounded her as he succumb to their passion.

Lucas didn't give Abigail a chance to pull away after she gave him the greatest pleasure he had ever received. He drew her up into his arms and plundered her lips. Each kiss drew longer and more passionate. He thought he might explode again from the sheer need consuming him with how tightly he held his emotions together. Each pull of his lips demanded Abigail's surrender. He refused to allow her even one minute to herself for fear she would regret her gift. Even if she were the one who had instigated the affection.

When he pulled her up to him, her nightgown had ridden up her thighs, leaving her softness bare. Her core pressed against him. The wetness displayed her need, making his cock harden again. His fingers drew out her moans with each slide in and out of her. While her wet core showed how excited she had grown from pleasuring him, it was nothing compared to how her body reacted to his touch. A warmth flowed over his fingers at her need.

Abigail expected nothing more from Lucas. She only wanted to give him pleasure with nothing in return. But when he pleasured her with each demand of his fingers, her body rejoiced and ached for him to satisfy the need consuming her soul. There were no words to describe the spiraling sensations sending her over the edge. She clung to Lucas with all her might, in fear she would fall and he wouldn't catch her. Her kisses grew frantic, and she tore at his shirt with the need to feel the heat from his skin against hers. Buttons flew in the air.

Lucas must have sensed her desperation or else he felt the same pull because her nightgown flew over her head in one swipe. The kiss they shared interrupted only briefly before they reclaimed each other's lips in frenzy. Abigail's hands raked across his chest before circling around to his back. She pressed her breasts against him and his heat surrounded her, wrapping her in a cocoon she never wanted to fly away from.

Abigail's body rocked against his fingers, drawing forth his need to have her unravel. He slid another finger inside her and moaned at the tightness. He drew them out slowly and waited. When Abigail tried to move, he gripped her hips, halting her movements.

Abigail whimpered. "Lucas."

Still, he held steady. He brushed his thumb across her clit, making her tremble. However, it was also his downfall when it pulsed a rapid beat of her need. Lucas released her hips to find her breast. He drew the tight nipple between his lips and sucked as his fingers plunged inside her sweet cunny.

Abigail's desire heightened with each stroke of his fingers. Each time he dipped deeper into her core, her pleasure exploded with a surge of wetness. She threw her head back, and he sucked greedily on her breasts. The buds melted on his tongue. Their sweetness begged for him to savor each puckered fruit as if they were the last berries to savor. His teeth scraped against her nipple when her hair swept across his thighs, teasing his cock.

Abigail's torment to have Lucas shake under her regard washed over her as her body shook from the same sensations. Lucas devoured her breasts like a starving man eating his last meal as his fingers built her need to an unbearable ache only he could appease. With each stroke, he wrung out her desire, only to build it to a higher level, leaving her unable to find release.

Abigail's hips moved in sync. Only she needed something more powerful to fulfill the ache binding her in a vice of an uncontrollable need. Lucas stilled at her unspoken plea. He lifted his head and his gaze pierced her. Abigail lost herself in the storm he held her under.

Lucas saw the need reflected in Abigail's gaze wrap around her in a fury of emotions beyond either of their control. When he slid inside her, he watched the fury calm and soften her features. He understood the desperation claiming her sanity since he suffered from the same affliction. However, once their bodies joined as one, every heightened emotion settled into a calm wave of forever.

Lucas wrapped his hands around Abigail's waist and guided her to move with him. With each stroke, their bodies forged a bond that neither of them would otherwise admit. But one Lucas wished to succumb to. He planned to throw himself into the madness surrounding them and hoped Abigail would join him.

Lucas kept Abigail's desperation at bay with gentle kisses while his body swayed with hers. No longer did her emotions suck her under. Instead, they blossomed in their lovemaking. With each rise of his hips, Abigail joined her body with his in a dance, claiming their love. Lucas calmed her soul. Because he was her other half and always would be.

Lucas pulled Abigail close and kissed her, slowly savoring their desire as their bodies trembled from the aftermath of passion. He closed his eyes and wrapped her in his embrace.

Neither of them whispered their undying declarations.

Chapter Fifteen

Abigail allowed herself the enjoyment of lying wrapped in Lucas's arms. The silence comforted her and gave her a brief glimpse of contentment. It may only last shortly, but Lucas's embrace offered her a sense of security she hadn't felt in a long while. However, the sunlight seeping into her bedchamber also spoke of their time ending.

Lucas's fingers stroked across Abigail's shoulder and along her back. "Will you dress and come with me?"

Abigail stilled. "Where?" she whispered.

Lucas continued with his caress. "For an early morning walk in the garden."

Abigail didn't want their time to end. "Yes."

Lucas released the breath he held with relief when she answered so readily. When she raised her head and offered him a shy smile, he couldn't help but smile in return. Which made Abigail blush a becoming shade of pink, only making his smile grow wider. She ducked her head and looked around on the floor. When he realized she looked to cover herself, he gave into her discomfort and draped the quilt around her shoulders.

Abigail rose off Lucas after he wrapped her in the quilt. His invitation had taken her by surprise, but she didn't want to part from him quite yet. His playful smile contradicted his attitude the past year, and she wished to savor it for as long as he chose to act in this regard.

She moved behind the dressing partition and pulled on a variety of layers of dress. When she lowered the walking dress over her hips, she realized how her giddiness of spending the early morning with Lucas invaded her senses. Did he feel the same way?

Abigail peeked out to see him wearing the same silly grin, waiting for her. She gulped at the sight of the wide expanse of his chest on display, remembering how her hands raked along his body. The contrast of the hardness of his body against her soft curves heightened the desire that still flickered for another round of fulfillment. Abigail pressed her cheek to the wooded panel in hopes it would cool her thoughts. Its roughness only scratched her cheek instead.

Lucas stood staring at the bed before him. He itched to discard his clothing and crawl between the sheets. Their union shared on the rickety chair had only soothed a flicker of his need. There was more he wished to enlighten Abigail on in the pleasures of lovemaking. Pleasures that would take hours, days, weeks, years, a lifetime to fulfill.

He turned when he heard the rustle of movement behind the dressing screen and grinned at her stare. It would appear Abigail's thoughts reflected the same need as his. However, they couldn't indulge in their desires. He held out his hand, and she glided over to him with a carefree regard he hadn't seen in her since she was a young girl.

Once she reached him, she turned and presented her back. "Will you be so kind and play lady's maid, good sir?"

Her teasing tone was the only thing that kept him from stripping off her clothes and throwing her onto the bed. With hands that shook, he buttoned her dress. His fingers lingered on the last button and his thumb brushed across the back of her creamy neck. He stole a kiss and pulled away, drawing her hand in his.

Lucas hurried them toward the mirror and into the secret passageway, not giving Abigail a chance to change her mind. He led them into his bedchamber and drew on a fresh shirt before ushering Abigail out again. Her soft laughter trailed behind them. Once he reached the latched door leading them out into the garden, he turned. Abigail's enjoyment shone brightly, teasing him to join in with her. He placed a soft kiss against her lips before opening the door.

Lucas guided her to a bench. "Wait here," he said before disappearing through the servant's entrance. No sooner had he entered than he exited with a linen tied with string.

Abigail tilted her head. "Did you steal those?"

Lucas winked at her and held out his hand again. Abigail placed her hand inside his and they walked deeper into the gardens. When Abigail thought they would stop and enjoy the delightful scent wafting from the linen, Lucas surprised her by walking farther. Once he stopped, Abigail realized where he had taken her. She hadn't visited this side of the garden lately. It was a place she had hidden away whenever the sense of not belonging overwhelmed her. And it was always Lucas who would coax her away, making her see the acceptance Colebourne tried to provide with his security. After a while, she no longer needed to hide but embraced her new family.

They settled on a bench, and Lucas unwrapped their breakfast. He wore a mischievous smile when she noticed the sweets he'd stolen. Covered in sugar were Cook's cream-filled pastries.

"You stole Ramsay's treats," Abigail accused, reaching for one and taking a bite.

Lucas laughed, popping one into his mouth. "Serves him right for getting special treatment when the rest of us get served the plain scones while he visits."

Abigail giggled. They ate the remaining in silence, shooting each other smiles in between bites. After they finished, they enjoyed the quiet early morning and watched the birds swoop in to take a drink from the fountain and fly off again. Abigail enjoyed the peacefulness with Lucas.

She couldn't blame the duke's matchmaking attempts on the distance placed between them. If she were to reflect on when their differences started, she would have to admit it was when Lucas began courting Selina. By then, she had fallen head over heels for Lucas and couldn't bear to watch their courtship.

Which was the reason for her to seek employment, a position she planned to keep, and Colebourne's invitation for Lord Ross to visit only made it more of a reality. Soon the fantasy she held of Lucas whisking her away to make her his bride would wither.

She struggled to keep her gaze off him and peeked out of the corner of her eye. Abigail wanted to etch every expression of him into her memories. Any moment she could steal with him to tuck away and treasure while alone. He ran his hand through his hair and appeared nervous. While he spoke nothing aloud, his lips moved in a private conversation with himself. She wondered what troubled him.

We must marry and I have the perfect solution. We can steal away to Gretna Green where nobody can find fault with our union because it is final. She would balk at that reasoning, Lucas argued with himself.

Abigail, will you marry me? No. His proposal should sound more romantic.

You are the love of my life and I wish to make you my bride. Yes. That sounded perfect. Should he go down on one knee? Or draw her into his arms?

Why was this so bloody difficult? They were both reasonable adults and Abigail must see the reason for such haste. She didn't need a flowery declaration. She was a sensible miss.

Lucas leapt to his feet and walked to the fountain. He dipped his fingers into the water to wash the sugar away. Then he strode back to the bench with determination to ask Abigail to marry him. She lifted her head, smiling at him with patience at his agitated state. He rubbed the back of his neck, his doubts keeping him silent. Every argument he held against asking for her hand in marriage before smacked him to a halt.

Each reason still held strong. The most important one of not wanting her to suffer the ton's snobbery and watching her happiness wither away almost kept him silent. But his father had raised him to be a gentleman. Since he'd taken her virtue and ruined her for any other man, that alone overruled any objections to making her his wife.

"We will marry immediately. Tonight, after everyone has gone to bed, we will leave for Gretna Green. Tomorrow you shall become my wife," Lucas stated.

Abigail's smile slipped away, and she sat in a daze. It was as if she witnessed this scene from a distance. One second, they were sharing a moment of utter joy, and the next, he ripped away her happiness by his coldhearted order. Lucas didn't even have the decency to show any ounce of emotion in his regard toward her. As if she were a problem that needed to be handled.

Abigail's lips pinched as she brushed the crumbs from her skirts. She rose with a dignity she was far from feeling and folded her hands in front of her. "No," she snarled.

Lucas jerked back at Abigail's vicious answer. "No?"

Abigail gritted her teeth, holding back the fury she wished to unleash. "No!"

Lucas frowned at her negative reply. On the second one, her voice rose a pitch higher. His pride objected and forced him to act without reason. "You have no other choice. I ruined you and we will wed. Once my father learns of our indiscretions, he will insist on our marriage."

Abigail raised an eyebrow. "Will you inform him?"

Lucas scoffed. "No. I am more of a gentleman than my fellow family members."

"Are you?" Abigail demanded. "Because from my viewpoint, you are a whole other level of a degenerated gentleman. One that far surpasses their ungentlemanly conduct. A scoundrel of the highest order."

Lucas, not recognizing Abigail's temper climbing, continued on with his offending proposal. "You must see reason. There is no alternative course for our relationship but one of marriage. There might be consequences for the past two evenings we shared. One that would leave you a branded woman."

Abigail arched an eyebrow. "Like my mother?"

"Exactly." Lucas regretted his answer the second he uttered the word. Abigail paled at his insult. "I apologize. I never meant to imply anything negative toward your mother. Please forgive me, Abigail," Lucas pleaded.

Abigail took a deep breath. But it didn't calm her any. Lucas's cruel words ignited her temper to a level where she could no longer hold back. She took a step forward and poked him in the chest. "You, my lord, are nothing but a pompous jackass who holds no clue how to treat a lady. Oh, but I forgot, I am not a lady. Am I, *Lord Gray*?"

She poked his chest again, this time pressing harder. "I am nothing but a lowly being who should hold nothing but gratitude that someone as high ranking as you has shown me any sort of attention."

Lucas tried to defend himself. "Abigail, you misunderstand."

"No, Lord Gray, I have not. Over the past year, you have made your opinion more than clear. I was a fool to think otherwise. A fool who imagined herself so deeply in love with you that I made excuses for your every action. Well, no more." Abigail curtsied to Lucas. "While I thank you for your *kind* offer, *my lord*, I must refuse. You see, I would rather be a fallen woman than a woman married to a man who holds no respect for her."

Abigail turned and rushed toward the manor. With every call of her name, she ran faster. She didn't stop until she closed the door to her bedroom. And then and only then did she allow the tears to fall. She never imagined Lucas would inflict so much pain upon her heart. But then his past actions had proven otherwise.

How was this incident any different?

Chapter Sixteen

Colebourne stared out the window, watching Abigail run as if the demons of hell were on her tail. Instead of demons, his insufferable son followed in her wake. He thought they would return with the news he had anxiously waited for when he saw them leave the manor at dawn with a glow of love surrounding them. However, the manner of Abigail's return only showed his son had offended his ward.

When will the boy ever learn? Colebourne was at his wit's end of making the match between Lucas and Abigail. He had never known such two stubborn souls. Each time he thought they were about to capitulate, one of them pulled away. Lucas's views on how his peers would accept Abigail were outdated. And Abigail's refusal to accept the value of herself irritated Colebourne. She held more empathy and kindness than any lady of the ton. He would hold nothing but honor at calling her his daughter-in-law. And by God, she would be. Even if he had to force them into a union.

Colebourne sat behind his desk and sighed in defeat. In all honesty, he could never force them into a marriage. He wanted them to understand how rare the depth of their love for each other was. How they would never meet another soul to share the love with. He needed his son to see how his entire family supported his union with Abigail and how they would stand up against those who would object. And he needed Abigail to see her worth and realize that the day he took her in, she had become a member of this family.

He needed Lucas and Abigail to love each other and realize how their love would overcome anything or anyone who stood in their way.

~~~~~~

Abigail curled into a ball under the quilt and wept over the loss of every fantasy she held ending with Lucas declaring his love. She didn't understand why the connection she felt with Lucas while they made love didn't carry over to their interactions outside of the bedroom. They had at one time. Why couldn't they recreate the bond they used to have when they were friends? Because during that time, Abigail had become aware that they shared more than simple friendship. Now she expected Lucas to treat her differently after the passion they shared between them.

"Ow!" Gemma exclaimed. "Abby, why do you have buttons scattered across the floor?"

In her grief, Abigail never heard Gemma enter. She swiped at her tears and held still, pretending to be asleep. However, she couldn't fool her friend. She knew Abigail too well. Still, Abigail tried, hoping Gemma would leave.

Gemma attempted to bend over to pick up the buttons. She had to rest her hand on the bed for balance. After gathering a few, she rose and turned them over in her hand. She gasped when she realized they weren't a lady's button but one from a gentleman's shirt. Gemma knew the difference since her husband's shirts held similar buttons. Which could only mean one thing. Her friend had entertained a gentleman in her room. Not any gentleman, the one who held her friend's heart. Lucas.

A smile swept across Gemma's face, displaying her joy at their union. The entire family had waited with eagerness for them to admit their love. She couldn't wait to share Abigail's happiness with everyone. However, Gemma sensed all was not well.

"Abby?" Gemma noticed Abigail stiffen under the covers and knew her friend tried to avoid her. Because if Abigail was asleep, she would've scattered the blankets across the floor and the bed would've appeared as if a storm struck it.

Gemma sighed. Lucas must have ruined the fragile bond and now her friend suffered heartache once again. She maneuvered herself to the opposite side of the bed and crawled under the quilt next to Abigail. She stroked Abigail's hair and whispered kind words of comfort. Abigail turned toward her with tears streaming down her cheeks.

"Ah, love," Gemma whispered at the heartbreak filling Abigail's eyes.

Gemma wiped at Abigail's tears, which only made her cry harder. She couldn't stop the flow of misery pouring from her soul. Lucas's idea of a proposal had broken what remained of her heart.

"I refuse to love him any longer," Abigail declared.

Gemma nodded. "Of course. He is an insufferable oaf who does not deserve your devotion. I shall have Barrett call him out for his scandalous behavior."

Abigail, lost in her thoughts, paid Gemma's comments no mind. "I was such a fool to believe he might love me. We shared a beautiful moment, and he treated me with such care. I thought I meant more to him than a lady he shared a tawdry affair with that made him feel guilty enough to demand we marry. Demand?" Abigail choked on the word that defined how Lucas viewed the outcome of their lovemaking.

Abigail's shoulders shook with a fresh wave of grief, and Gemma tried her best to offer her friend comfort. But no amount of sentiments would cure the damage Lucas had inflicted on Abigail with his cruel attempt at proposing. Gemma couldn't wait to inform her cousins and Selina of Lucas's mishap. They would make him suffer for his incompetence.

Once Abigail calmed, Gemma attempted to make her understand how much she valued her. "Do you remember when we lost our mothers and first came to Colebourne Manor?"

When Abigail nodded, Gemma continued. "We would crawl in each other's beds every night for the first two years and cry over our sorrow. Over time, the heartache grew more bearable to endure because of the friendship we shared. While our sadness remained and always would, it was because of you that I was able to smile every day. I made a solemn vow to ensure you the same happiness I found."

Abigail sniffled. "You are the sister I never had, and I love you. But 'tis not your duty but my own to fulfill."

Gemma brushed back Abigail's hair. "Then how may I help?"

Abigail attempted a smile. "Help me prepare for my journey to Lord Ross's estate."

While Abigail's request was the last thing Gemma wanted to do, she agreed. She only hoped her cousin came to his senses and corrected the errors of his way. "Only if you help roll me out of this bed first."

Abigail laughed at Gemma's attempt at humor. "Please. You are as dainty as ever."

Gemma frowned at her stomach. "I am a whale."

"Perhaps so," Abigail teased, reaching out to help Gemma. "But a loveable one who Ralston adores."

Gemma beamed at the mention of her husband. "As much as I adore him."

Abigail watched Gemma radiate with joy, and it warmed her heart to the love Gemma had found with Ralston. Her friend deserved the moon and stars, and she lived a life filled with love. As much as she wished the same for herself, Abigail found comfort in the happiness her family had captured the past year.

One day, she hoped she found the same.

~~~~~~

An hour had passed before Gemma stole away to join the other ladies for breakfast. Once Abigail calmed down, she had called for a bath for her. Abigail grew sleepy during the bath and wanted to lie for a spell. Gemma promised her she would return after luncheon to help her pack for the journey. Abigail clung to Gemma's hand until she drifted off to sleep. Gemma hated to leave her, but she needed to talk with everyone while they gathered together. It would make it too difficult to talk to them separately without being disturbed by each other's husbands or Uncle Theo and Aunt Susanna for that matter.

Gemma strolled into Jacqueline's room and sat next to Selina on the chaise. Her friend smiled at her but continued on with her conversation with Charlie. They discussed Selina's life in Scotland while Jacqueline and Evelyn decided on names for Jacqueline's baby. Gemma laughed at some of the silly choices. She didn't interject herself into either conversation but waited for them to notice Abigail didn't join them. Which would be any second now.

Evelyn paused, glancing toward the door. "Is Abigail not going to join us?"

Gemma shook her head. "Nay."

Jacqueline frowned. "Why ever not?"

The other conversation stopped once they realized Gemma held information to share. Gemma smoothed her skirt before opening her palm.

She spread out the buttons and placed them in a circle. Each of the ladies held a bewildered look at her actions.

"Why are you clutching those buttons? Do you plan on sewing this morning?" Charlie asked. "If so, I am taking myself off to the stables."

Selina leaned forward and drew a button out of Gemma's hand, inspecting the quality and size. She quirked a brow. "Is there a reason you need to repair your husband's shirt?"

Gemma smirked. "'Tis not from my husband."

Charlie tilted her head as she tried to understand the mystery behind the buttons. "If they are not Ralston's buttons, then to whom might they belong?"

A mischievous smile lit Selina's face. "Lucas," she guessed.

Gemma nodded with a frown. "Yes."

"Your answer does not sound promising for Abigail," Evelyn observed.

"Because our cousin has once again blundered his attempt to win Abigail's heart," Gemma stated, rubbing her stomach.

Selina frowned at Gemma's distress. She stood and urged Gemma back against the cushions, drawing her legs on the chaise. Evelyn handed Selina a blanket, and Selina drew it over Gemma. "Calm down."

Gemma took a deep breath. "When will he ever learn?"

"What has he done now?" Jacqueline asked.

"It is more than obvious what Lucas has done," Charlie quipped.

"Charlotte," Evelyn warned.

Charlie shrugged. "What? Obviously, he seduced Abigail, if the buttons are any indication. Am I correct?"

Gemma nodded.

"Is he refusing to marry her?" Evelyn asked.

Gemma's lips twisted in her indecision on how to answer the question. "Not exactly."

Charlie rose with her hands on her hips. "Explain."

"He stole her away to the garden this morning in a romantic gesture to the spot she used to hide when we first moved here."

"The spot Lucas would coax her out of by promising her we were her family now?" Jacqueline inquired.

"The very one."

Evelyn looked confused. "It sounds romantic."

"It was until Lucas opened his mouth to demand they wed. Then proceeded to explain how if anyone learned of their tryst, a stigma would follow in her wake if she refused him."

"That arrogant arse. Did he even realize he offended Abigail's mother with his rambling proposal?" Charlie demanded.

Gemma shrugged. She held no clue what Lucas's intentions or thoughts were with his proposal. Nor was she to guess what he meant.

"I am going to string him by his bollocks," Selina threatened.

Each lady quivered at the venomous tone of Selina's threat. The blonde-haired beauty stood with fire flashing in her eyes, once again reminding them of when they referred to her as a shrew. As an enemy, Selina was most vicious, but as a friend, her viciousness kept her friends protected. They actually feared for their cousin's life if Selina decided to act on her fury.

Charlie attempted to lighten the mood. "It would seem as if you adapted to the barbarian lifestyle of your husband's ancestors during your stay in Scotland."

However, Selina would no longer stay silent. "I promised Lucas to keep quiet on his deceit with his promise to make right by Abigail. But his actions have displayed nothing but his ability to remain a fool who at every turn breaks Abigail's heart. Well, no more. I will seek my revenge and he will rue the day he ever crossed my path."

Charlie and Evelyn exchanged a look. They knew they needed to calm Selina before Gemma and Jacqueline grew more agitated. The stress wasn't good for either lady or the babies they carried. Charlie guided Selina to take a seat, and Evelyn prepared a cup of tea for her.

"What are Abigail's plans?" Charlie asked Gemma, trying to distract everyone from Selina's tirade.

"She wishes to prepare for her governess position with Lord Ross. I told her I would help her pack this afternoon."

"Pshh. Governess position." Selina shook her head in disgust.

Gemma's eyebrows drew together. "Yes. She wishes to convince Lord Ross to leave shortly after his arrival. And at this point, I agree with her and promised Abigail my support."

"And if there is no Lord Ross to arrive?" Selina mumbled.

"Why would he not arrive? He promised Abigail a position and Uncle Theo vetted him to be a reliable gentleman that Abigail could depend upon," Gemma argued.

"So I have heard," Selina replied. "But what if he is not real?"

"You should not joke about such things. It is unkind," Jacqueline reprimanded her.

"Are you aware of the various titles my husband will acquire once he becomes a duke?" Selina asked.

Charlie scoffed. "More than we can count."

Selina set her cup of tea on the table. "Shall I name a few of them or perhaps the only one which matters?"

Charlie threw her hands in the air. "I do not see how Duncan's status once he becomes a duke matters at this moment. We are discussing Abigail's plans."

Evelyn gasped and covered her hand over her mouth. "Lord Ross?"

Selina nodded once she finally forced one of them to understand the dilemma unfolding. "Yes."

Jacqueline's eyes widened at the truth coming to light. "His two children are Anna and Rose."

"Are those not Aunt Olivia and Susanna's middle names?" Charlie asked.

"Oh, no. Please tell me Lucas is not Lord Ross," Gemma cried out.

Selina cringed at the distress coming from each lady. "I wish I could."

"How did we miss the signs? Abigail has told us of Lord Ross and his children. Why did we not recognize the similarities sooner?" Gemma wondered.

Evelyn looked around the room before answering what everyone else was thinking. "Because our own happiness clouded Abigail's misery. We have failed Abigail."

Charlie stood with her arms crossed, observing Selina with her head tilted to the side. "How long have you known?"

Selina sat up straighter. "I only figured it out yesterday."

Charlie narrowed her gaze. "Why did you not expose Lucas and his lies before now?"

Selina sighed in defeat. "Because at first I thought it was one of Uncle Theo's mad matchmaking ploys. I confronted him and Mama and they assured me it was harmless and they would stop."

"Instead, they continued with the madness and plotted to invite the mysterious Lord Ross for a visit," Jacqueline mused.

Selina nodded. "After dinner, Duncan wanted to check on Lucas since he left the table abruptly. While I walked with Abigail to the drawing room, she decided to retire to her bedchamber. I decided to join Duncan and found him arguing with Lucas. While eavesdropping, I learned of Lucas's deceit. He promised to send Abigail a letter to withdraw his offer. I never intended for Abigail to get hurt." Selina twisted her hands together.

Charlie slashed her hand through the air. "Of course you didn't. You were only trying to protect Abigail. 'Tis not your fault. No. The blame lies with Lucas and two matchmakers who need to be taught a lesson."

Evelyn jumped to her feet and started pacing back and forth. Charlie frowned at her sister. Usually, Evelyn would sit quietly, waiting for someone else to decide on the course of action they would take. However, her sister would become the mastermind of revenge for this task if her fierce expression reflected her plan.

"Evelyn?" Charlie tried to get her attention.

Evelyn held up a finger, then continued her pacing. "We must teach every individual involved a lesson."

"Agreed," Jacqueline said.

Charlie smirked. "And how shall we accomplish that, dear sister?"

Evelyn stopped and quirked an eyebrow at Charlie's sarcasm. "Why, with Lord Ross and his two daughters. Who else?"

Jacqueline frowned. "Dear, we have already established that Lord Ross is a false character created by Lucas."

Evelyn smiled serenely. "Yes, I am well aware. However, if Lord Ross were to arrive, it would expose Lucas's lies and the manipulations of Uncle Theo and Aunt Susanna."

Charlie glanced toward the other ladies, pleading for their help. When none of them offered her any help, she walked over to Evelyn and guided her to sit back down. "Of course, dear. Your plan sounds excellent."

Evelyn brushed away Charlie's handling. "Stop placating me and allow me to explain my plan."

Gemma laughed at Evelyn's determination for the impossible. "Yes, Charlie. Leave Evelyn alone. I am very curious to learn how she plans to lure a fictional character for a visit to teach Lucas a lesson."

Evelyn glared at Gemma. "Never underestimate me, dear cousin."

Gemma bit back another giggle. "I would never dream to."

Selina's eyes twinkled at their exchange. "Evelyn has developed a backbone with her marriage to Worthington. I am most impressed."

Evelyn nodded. "Thank you."

Jacqueline huffed. "If you children are finished, I would like to hear what Evelyn has planned. Charlie, please sit, you are working my nerves with your agitation."

Charlie followed Jaqueline's directions and sat on the bed, waiting for Evelyn to inform them of her plan. "You may begin."

Evelyn folded her hands in her lap. "Is Sinclair's cousin still set to arrive for a visit today?"

"Yes. But I do not understand how his visit is important," Charlie stated.

"Your mother-in-law informed me he has taken to acting in small plays in his village."

"Yes, his daughters fancy themselves on stage. So he indulges them by allowing them small parts, and he joins the cast to supervise them when the traveling tropes pass through," Charlie explained.

Evelyn nodded in satisfaction. "Do you think they would enjoy partaking in a play where they perform the lead parts?"

"Why, you are the devious twin, not Charlie," Selina whispered.

Charlie laughed. "Why, I think she is."

Jacqueline shifted in her chair. "This might work. But we will need the letters Lucas and Abigail exchanged between them."

"I can gather Abigail's letters when I help her this afternoon," Gemma offered.

"And I will enlist Duncan's help in securing Lucas's letters as Lord Ross," Selina said.

"Excellent. Do you think Sinclair's cousin will agree?" Evelyn asked.

Charlie nodded with enthusiasm. "Yes. If not, then his daughters will persuade him to do so."

Evelyn rubbed her hands together. "Then, ladies, I think we have a start in our attempt to teach a lesson. But most of all, we must succeed. Because I fear it is our last chance to make a match between Lucas and Abigail. Shall we make a solid plan to achieve the most precious outcome of all? Love."

Everyone agreed, and they spent the morning plotting the final act for the matchmaking madness they had all endured over the past year. They each wished for Abigail and Lucas to declare their everlasting love to one another.

After all, loving another soul was the most passionate madness of all.

Chapter Seventeen

Gray followed the other gentlemen on his horse. When they approached him this morning for an afternoon of fishing, they had refused his answer of no. Every excuse he gave them, they refuted until he accepted their invitation. It wasn't as if he didn't enjoy their company; it was because, over the past two days of enduring silence from Abigail and his cousins, he didn't wish to be in the company of others.

Even Selina glared at him whenever he came across her. When he tried to engage her in a conversation, she gave him the cut direct as if they were in a ballroom filled with others. She acted most bizarre. But he knew better than to comment on her behavior. Duncan would make him regret anything negative he spoke, cousin or not.

And that was also his predicament with every other gentleman present. They would make his existence miserable if he even so much as complained about their wives' treatment. He understood the reason for their unsympathetic behavior and he only had himself to blame. By now, he was positive Abigail had told them of his bungled marriage proposal.

A proposal he regretted the moment he asked. Not that he regretted proposing. No. His regret lay with the words that spewed from his mouth. Instead of demanding they marry and slandering her mother, he should have declared his love. If he could get Abigail alone, he knew she would accept the marriage proposal he planned. However, at his every attempt to speak with Abigail, his cousins instigated themselves and drew her away. He even tried the secret passageway, but the door to her bedchamber wouldn't budge. He didn't dare approach her through the door in the hallway because of who might notice.

Damn his meddling cousins. They were as bad as his father and Aunt Susanna. He thought he might have Uncle Ramsay on his side, but his uncle kept shaking his head in disapproval.

While his friends settled around the pond, Gray stalked over to the opposite side and settled against a rock. He threw the pole out, watched the line float against the wind, and listened to the snippets of conversations drifting across to him. They discussed a range of topics. Everything from Gemma's and Jacqueline's pregnancies to Ralston and Kincaid's business venture. He didn't envy any one of them but held pride in their happiness and success.

However, with each minute he sat away from them, he realized perhaps he was envious. He wanted all of that for himself but held no clue on how to make it happen.

He rose and walked back toward them, leaving his pole in the water. His friends stopped talking and stared at him with interest and a bit of skepticism when he reached them.

Gray lifted his hands in the air in defeat. "Tell me how."

He figured since he asked them for their help, they would offer it freely. However, he was mistaken.

Sinclair smirked. "How what, exactly?"

"Do you wish to learn which bait works best to catch a fish?" Ralston asked.

Worthington winced. "From what I understand, his timing is off. He is not using the correct line."

Kincaid shook his head. "You are correct about the line. But I believe it is also in his approach when he casts the line."

Gray gritted his teeth and bit his tongue. Apparently, they wouldn't help him until he allowed them their bit of amusement at his expense.

Forrester laughed. "Each of you has made a fine point. However, he will never catch the lady if he continues to lure her like he fishes. You must not compare catching a lady to how one would catch a fish."

"You must charm her," Sinclair suggested.

Worthington nodded. "You must show her how hard you have fallen."

Ralston smiled wickedly. "Tempt her."

Forrester's lips twisted into a smile. "Steal her away."

Kincaid quirked an eyebrow. "And seduce her. Or better yet, have her seduce you."

Gray harrumphed. "She will not even speak to me, let alone seduce me."

Kincaid shrugged. "She might surprise you."

Gray rolled his eyes. "While I appreciate your advice, none of your suggestions will help me in winning over Abigail."

"Do you hope to win her over because you love her or because you are fulfilling your obligation of a gentleman?" Sinclair asked.

"Why cannot it be for both reasons?"

"Because Abigail deserves more than what you are offering her," Sinclair explained.

Gray ran his hands through his hair. "How can I win her love when your wives run interference? They will not allow me a moment alone with her."

Ralston chuckled. "You grew up with them. You should know how to be more devious than them."

"One would think," Gray mumbled.

Every one of them understood how each lady could sweet-talk their way out of any situation or crook their little finger to get their way. Even Gray fell for their charm. Plus, you never double-crossed any of them. Because when they struck their revenge, they allowed no mercy.

"Perhaps you can keep your wives distracted while I convince Abigail to marry me."

Each of them shook their heads in denial.

"Sorry, mate." Kincaid slapped Lucas on the shoulder.

Worthington gathered his pole from the water. "We made our wives a promise."

"But we can offer you advice," Forrester added. "Instead of expecting Abigail to feel gratitude for receiving a proposal from you, be honest with her. Forget about everyone else's opinion and focus on the unique woman in front of you. Who, for whatever reason we have yet to figure out, loves you unconditionally. Arrogance and all."

Gray narrowed his gaze. "I am not arrogant."

Forrester shrugged. "Perhaps not. But you are uptight and too worried about the strict structure of society."

"Those guidelines are set for a purpose," Gray argued.

"For whom?" Sinclair asked.

"For every single one of us and our generations to come."

Kincaid nodded. "And Abigail is not worthy enough to be included with those standards."

Gray advanced on his friend. "She is more worthy than anyone I know. How dare you insult her so."

Kincaid held his hands up and backed away. "I am only stating my opinion from your marriage proposal and the way you have treated her of late."

Gray halted. Kincaid's comment sank in. Had he been so callous in his regard toward Abigail? He closed his eyes. When he opened them again, it was to see his friends watching him come to terms with his behavior. All along, they had tried to make him see reason, only for him to brush their comments aside. It was a wonder Abigail even acknowledged him.

"I have been a fool."

"Finally, I did not believe you would ever see the light," Sinclair quipped.

"How do I convince Abigail of my sincerity?"

"Humble yourself at her mercy," Worthington answered.

"And if that does not work?"

"You will not know unless you try," Ralston encouraged him.

"You are correct." Gray strode to his horse. He paused and turned around, nodding to the other gentlemen. "Thank you."

Each of them nodded. Gray rode off, and they watched him with amusement.

"Do you imagine he has a chance?" Kincaid asked.

Forrester laughed. "He might, but hopefully the lass makes him suffer for a bit."

The rest of the gentlemen laughed and returned to their fishing. After all, they had accomplished what their wives requested of them. They figured they would enjoy the peace before all hell erupted later. The plan their wives concocted only had one outcome, and that was a catastrophe.

But in truth, the madness of it all would prevail.

Chapter Eighteen

Lucas sat across from Abigail during dinner. He hadn't been able to convince Aunt Susanna to sit him next to Abigail for the meal. However, sitting across from her was the next best thing. It gave him a chance to see her since she avoided him at all costs. And now that he understood why, he didn't blame her in the slightest. He only hoped she would allow him to redeem himself.

Hopefully, for the rest of their lives together.

Worthington had mentioned for him to humble himself, but Lucas realized he would have to grovel at Abigail's feet for an ounce of forgiveness.

He watched her as she conversed with Duncan and Ralston. Although both gentlemen were happily married, it still didn't stop the jealousy coursing through him whenever she smiled at them. When her twinkling laughter drifted across to him, he scowled in annoyance.

"Careful, cousin, one would think Abigail meant more to you than a mistake needing to be rectified," Charlie baited him.

Lucas's scowl deepened. "She has never been a mistake."

"Mmm. Your marriage proposal spoke otherwise."

Lucas shot Charlie a glare. "I thought I told you to mind your own business. Why are you always placed next to me?"

"Yes, I seem to recall that order. However, I cannot. Also, I requested for Aunt Susanna to sit me next to you." Charlie smirked.

"Why?"

Charlie waggled her eyebrows. "You will see," she answered before turning back to Worthington.

Before he could question her further, Charlie started drilling Worthington about the horse she had gifted him as a wedding present. Once Charlie started talking about horses, no one would get a word in edgewise. When Abigail giggled, his head swiveled to discover what amused her, Charlie's comment already forgotten.

Abigail's cheeks warmed at Duncan's compliment. "You, sir, are an incorrigible flirt."

Duncan winked. "And you, lass, are as bonny as the blush that graces your cheeks."

Abigail couldn't stop giggling. Duncan's flirting had lifted her spirits. "Did Selina put you up to this?"

Duncan clutched at his heart. "What? A gentleman cannot compliment his lovely dinner companion?"

Abigail glanced across the table at Selina and saw her amusement at her husband's antics. Selina shrugged. "He is your trouble for this evening."

Abigail nodded her acceptance. Her friends' attempts to lighten her mood warmed her heart. Ever since Lucas proposed as if she were a burden, Abigail had sunk into a depression. When Lucas never attempted to apologize or offer for her hand again, Abigail had resigned herself to accepting the path fate laid out for her.

When Abigail looked away from Selina, her gaze clashed with Lucas. The smile slipped from her face at the emotions she saw gathered in the depths of his gaze. They conflicted with every word he spoke to her. She must be mistaken.

She glanced away, but her curiosity won out. When she glanced back at him, a permanent scowl had settled on his face. Abigail thought Lucas directed his irritation at her, but his eyes shot daggers at Duncan instead.

Duncan chuckled next to her and raised his glass toward Lucas in a silent toast. "I love ruffling the ole boy's feathers."

"And here I thought I was a captivating dinner companion," Abigail mumbled.

"You are at that, lass. But the English stick must suffer for his callous disregard."

Abigail took a sip of her wine. "It is of no use."

"I disagree. Forrester has caused Gray to blow smoke," Ralston interjected.

Forrester chuckled. "A most becoming sight, if I say so myself."

"My compliments." Ralston focused his gaze on Abigail. "If Forrester has not mentioned it this evening, please allow me to do so. The lovely shade of your dress brings out the gold flecks in your eyes. You absolutely sparkle this evening."

Abigail felt her cheeks warm again. "You are too kind."

"Nonsense. I only speak the truth."

Abigail smoothed a hand down her sleeve. "I had hoped Lord Ross would have arrived by now. I wanted to impress him."

Ralston nodded. "And you will."

Gray stilled when Abigail spoke of Lord Ross. In his mess of asking Abigail to marry him, he had forgotten to send her a missive withdrawing his offer. Now Abigail and his family waited for the earl to join them.

"You were supposed to write an explanation to Abigail," Selina hissed.

"I forgot," Gray whispered back.

"How could you forget something so simple?" Selina demanded.

Gray looked at Selina in exasperation. "Nothing concerning Abigail Cason is simple."

What Gray didn't realize was how loud his voice rose when he answered Selina. The table grew eerily quiet, making Lucas aware that everyone had heard him. His gaze swung to Abigail, and he watched her bright red cheeks pale, highlighting the light dusting of freckles.

Lucas's insult shouldn't have shocked Abigail. However, it did. It rocked her emotions to the core. Just when she thought she could handle his rejection and she was immune to him, he destroyed her all over again.

She fumbled with her napkin, dropping it to the floor in her haste to flee. Forrester and Ralston rose at the same time and helped her to stand.

Lucas jumped to his feet. "Abigail, you misunderstood what I meant."

Abigail lifted her chin. "I do not believe I do, Lord Gray. You have made yourself quite clear where I am concerned."

Colebourne pounded his fist on the table. "Sit down. It is past time we discuss the misconceptions surrounding your courtship."

Abigail looked at the duke in disbelief. "There is no courtship."

"Yes, there is," Lucas and Colebourne spoke at once.

Abigail sank into her chair. "This family is mad."

"On that we will agree, my girl." A gentleman spoke from the doorway.

"Father," Susanna exclaimed, rushing over to hug the Duke of Brockway.

"Susanna, dear." The gentleman returned her hug. "I see you are continuing your mischief with your sister's husband."

Susanna laughed, guiding her father to sit next to her. "Nonsense."

"Theo." He nodded at Colebourne but shook his head at Ramsay. "I thought you were wiser than to involve yourself with their mischief."

"I am only here fer the pastries," Ramsay answered.

"Oakes, please set a plate for my father," Susanna directed.

"Shall I also set places for the other visitors?" Oakes inquired.

Susanna looked confused. "Who did you bring along with you?"

"No one. Lord Ross and his daughters arrived when I did. Please show them in, Oakes. I wish to get acquainted with them," Brockway ordered.

The table grew quiet once again at the duke's arrival. The ladies exchanged panicked looks while their husbands shook their heads at the disaster ahead of them. Colebourne and Susanna exchanged puzzled expressions at the mention of Lord Ross. They had expected Brockway's arrival because of the detailed letter Susanna wrote to her father and Colebourne's plea for the duke to talk some sense into Lucas. However, it would appear there was more amiss than they planned.

Gray tried to get Duncan's attention, only for his cousin to avoid any eye contact with him. He turned to Selina to have her help make sense of a fictional gentleman's arrival, but she avoided him too. However, Charlie cackled her delight at his dilemma.

"What are you about?" Gray snarled.

Charlie placed her hand against her chest, aghast at his tone. "Why, nothing, dear cousin. Are you accusing me otherwise?" Her eyes sparkled with mischief.

"I damn well am. Come clean."

"Gray! You overstep with your tone with my wife," Sinclair declared from across the table.

Before Lucas could defend his tone, two young girls rushed into the dining room, followed by a distinguished-looking gentleman. His clothing was immaculate, befitting an earl, and his mannerism spoke of class. He smiled at his daughters' enthusiasm, causing every lady at the table to awe over his loving attitude. When he turned the smile onto them, each lady tittered a welcoming response. They acted like schoolgirls under his charm. Even Abigail fell for him. She rose and wiped her hands along her skirts, like she always did when she was nervous.

Who is this imposter?

If Abigail wasn't so much in love with the oaf sitting across from her, she could easily fall for Lord Ross. The gentle smile he directed at his daughters caused her heart to flutter. Not to mention the way his breathtaking eyes focused his attention on her. She never imagined the gentleman she had corresponded with all these months to hold this effect on her. While their letters bordered on the cusp of tender emotion, her heart had stubbornly remained devoted to Lucas. A devotion that kept leading to heartache.

"Miss Cason?" His deep voice brought Abigail to attention.

Abigail shook herself from her musings and dropped into a curtsy. "Lord Ross, how kind of you to accept the duke's invitation."

His smile deepened. "It was my pleasure. Anna, Rose, come and meet Miss Cason."

Abigail melted under his kind attention. "It is wonderful to meet you," she addressed the children.

Each girl grabbed onto one of Abigail's hands. "You are so beautiful," the youngest gushed.

Abigail knelt to their level. "Thank you. You girls are lovely too."

The servants bustled in, making room at the table for the additional guests. Since Colebourne had always allowed the girls and Lucas to eat at the dining room table when they were younger, it was not odd for him to allow Lord Ross's daughters the same privilege. Abigail helped them to settle next to their father.

"Rose and Anna? Hmm," Brockway stated.

"Yes. Their mother named them," Lord Ross explained.

"Where might Lady Ross be?" Brockway inquired.

Lord Ross frowned. "She passed away years ago."

Brockway nodded in understanding. "My condolences. Might I ask your late wife's name?"

Lord Ross, clueless to the heightened tension surrounding the room, answered, "Julia."

Silence awaited Brockway's reply. When he burst into laughter, it surprised everyone. "I am unsure who is behind this madness, but I must say, it is most brilliant. Now that I've played along, I must insist for this game to end. Although I am eager to hear your confessions."

When no one spoke up to explain, Abigail cleared her throat. "I am sorry, Your Grace. What is it you wish explained?"

Brockway pointed at Lord Ross. "Who this imposter might be?"

Abigail sat up straighter in her chair and explained Lord Ross's presence. "Lord Ross is no imposter. I have been corresponding with him for a few months. He is an earl who has offered me a governess position for his two daughters. Colebourne invited him to become better acquainted before I left to join Lord Ross's household."

Brockway tapped his fingers on the table as his shrewd gaze swept the table and eventually landed on Lucas. "Do you have something you wish to tell the girl?"

Lucas shook his head, refusing to answer his grandfather. He didn't want to make his confession in a room filled with his family members. He preferred to explain his deceit to Abigail alone.

Lucas rose. "Abigail, may I speak with you in private?"

"No." Her firm answer surprised not only him, but everyone else, too. "It is obvious everyone holds a secret I am oblivious to. If someone would be so kind as to explain why the duke is under the impression Lord Ross is an imposter."

"I can explain part of the deception if you will give me a chance," Lucas pleaded.

Abigail folded her hands in her lap. "I prefer not to be alone with you."

A thunderous expression crossed Lucas's face at Abigail's rejection. He had hoped to apologize for his deception and plead her forgiveness, but her stubbornness injured his pride. "I have no clue who this gentleman is because Lord Ross does not exist."

Brockway cleared his throat. "I beg to differ."

"Excuse me." He swept his arm toward his grandfather. "Abigail, allow me to introduce you to Lord Ross. It is a title my grandfather holds that will pass onto Duncan."

Abigail glanced between the gentleman posing as Lord Ross and the duke. "If you are not Lord Ross, then who are you?"

Sinclair winced. "My cousin, Benjamin, and the two young girls are his daughters, Victoria and Chloe."

"I am confused now more than ever."

Abigail's bewilderment caused everyone to cringe at their deceit. While some of them meant to teach Lucas a lesson, they never understood how deeply they would hurt Abigail in their ploy.

"I am the one who wrote you the letters, pretending to be Lord Ross," Lucas confessed.

Abigail went deadly still. "Why?"

"Because you were slipping away. I had hoped you would never follow through with accepting the false position. But over time, I grew envious of the connection we shared through our letters. I wished for you to share your thoughts with me, not Lord Ross. After Father had taken ill, we grew closer. I was under the impression you would refuse Lord Ross's offer, but you never did. I grew desperate," Lucas explained.

Abigail pointed at Sinclair's cousin. "And this gentleman?"

"We wanted to teach Lucas, Uncle Theo, and Aunt Susanna a lesson," Charlie confessed.

"I am such a fool," Abigail cried.

"No!" Everyone around the table tried to reassure her.

Abigail stumbled to her feet and fled the room. She didn't wish to hear any more of the deception. She had thought these people were her family and they loved her. But their actions proved otherwise. She never belonged and she never would.

With tears clouding her vision, she ran deeper into the garden, hiding away from their prying eyes. Once out of breath, she looked around and noticed she arrived at the very spot where Lucas proposed to her.

Abigail's breath hitched with a tear-wrenched sob that racked her body with shudders. She sank to the ground and laid her head on the bench and poured out her soul. Every tear she cried expressed the anguish tearing her soul apart.

Every single one of them had deceived her. With their determination to become the victor of a game out of control, they never stopped to realize how their ploys would hurt her. Even though she knew they meant well, it didn't lessen the pain any. She wished to run away but had nowhere to run to.

She had so many questions, but she didn't trust anyone to answer them truthfully. Which only left her to wonder . . .

Why does the act of love leave one feeling so raw?

Chapter Nineteen

Lucas rushed after Abigail, but his father's demand stopped him. "Leave her be."

Lucas swung around. "I cannot. I must explain my reasons. She is too vulnerable to be alone."

Susanna rose and urged Lucas to sit down. "Abigail needs to calm down before you approach her. If you catch her now, each of you will express emotions that cannot be unspoken. Words each of you might regret. Trust me, dear."

Lucas sat down, defeated. He knew his aunt's words to be true, but it didn't lessen his need to find Abigail. The pain reflected in her gaze had shaken her body, too. He wanted to hold her while she cried out her sorrow. Then he wanted to grovel at her feet for forgiveness. After she calmed, he would profess his undying love and pray she still loved him.

Sinclair's cousin rose. "If you will excuse us, we shall take our leave and allow you to settle your family matter."

Benjamin ushered his daughters out of the dining room. Selina watched them go and guilt settled in her heart for her part in the deception. With determination to make amends for Abigail's sake, she would explain the part she had played. She only hoped once Abigail learned the truth, she would still consider her a friend.

Selina slid the knife back and forth on the linen tablecloth, mesmerized by the glide of the blade. The candlelight flickered against the silver, casting a glow to reflect off and bounce around. She began her confession. "While I wasn't the one to start the downfall of this fiasco, I will take the blame for the part I played in its catastrophe."

"Love, you are not to blame," Duncan reassured Selina.

"Let her speak. No one else is forthcoming," Brockway demanded.

Selina stopped playing with the knife and raised her head. She faced the duke and continued. "When Abigail told me of the position Lord Ross offered her and mentioned her two young charges, their names sounded familiar. Once I pieced together the familiarity, I grew convinced it was the works of Theo and Susanna and their matchmaking mischief. When I confronted them, they confessed their involvement. However, they played me false, as I learned after I overheard a conversation between Lucas and Duncan, where Lucas confessed to be the one responsible for deceiving Abigail all these months."

"Do you have anything to share?" Colebourne asked Lucas.

Lucas stayed silent. He had much to share, but he would only make his confession to Abigail. She deserved to hear the reasons behind his actions before anyone else.

When Lucas still didn't speak, Selina finished explaining her involvement. "Lucas promised to write a letter to Abigail that explained the position was no longer available and his refusal to accept the duke's offer to visit Colebourne Manor. When he proposed to Abigail and slandered her character, I sought revenge and convinced the other ladies to help me seek justice for Abigail. However, it backfired and has left Abigail heartbroken."

Colebourne rose. "The fault lies with no one except for myself. I started this drama a year ago and allowed it to escalate out of my control. My greatest wish was for everyone to find happiness. While I found success with my wards, I failed my son. Instead of allowing him to make his own mistakes in life, I tried to force him into admitting his love for someone who was not his ideal mate. For that I apologize."

Colebourne lifted his glass in a toast. "What I am about to admit contradicts my apology. But I wish to applaud everyone's efforts in trying to make this match. It only shows the dedication this family possesses to make Abigail a permanent member. I appreciate the creativity you ladies added to the mix. You might have made a success out of it, if it were not for my letter to Brockway to invite him here in hopes he could convince Lucas what a mistake he made by refusing Abigail as his soul mate."

Lucas barked out a laugh. "If every single meddling busybody would have minded their own business, Abigail and I might be celebrating our engagement."

"Sure you would, boy. You have the same fumbling finesse your father possesses," Ramsay quipped.

Brockway laughed. "Ahh, I see the similarities. Do you remember the time when Colebourne swept Olivia through a dance right into the refreshment table, drenching her white dress in red punch? Then he had the audacity to blame the entire incident on her in front of the entire ton."

Colebourne cringed. "Yet she still said yes."

Brockway nodded. His focus landed on Lucas. "Yes, she did."

While the story of his parents' courtship should give him hope with Abigail, it compared nothing to the tribulations that kept them apart. Everyone thought it was as simple as confessing his love, but he feared his deceit overruled the simple act of love. He no longer held onto any hope and he wouldn't blame Abigail if she never forgave him. Because he couldn't forgive himself for the anguish he had caused her.

If only he had opened his eyes sooner. Every couple in this room had overcome obstacles to have successful marriages. And they had achieved success because they stood by each other and fought against their demons together, while he had used the reasons they needed to fight as excuses to keep them apart. And for what reason?

Did he care if the members of the ton supported his marriage? Abigail held more worth than any lady he had ever met. In his attempt to protect her, it had kept him from confessing his love. Yes, the vipers would whisper about Abigail behind her back, and the snakes would slither around, attempting to seduce her. But he had forgotten the power his father held and the power that would transfer to him when, God forbid, his father passed. Not to mention the power of his family members who would stand behind their union.

Now his doubts and reasons seemed foolish to begin with. By denying his love for Abigail, he had only shown her how she was an embarrassment to him. When in truth he held nothing but pride for her.

"Excuse me." Lucas never waited for a reply and rushed away. He needed to find Abigail before it was too late.

"Is there any hope for them?" Susanna whispered.

"Yes," Colebourne answered firmly, expressing his belief in Lucas and Abigail's love.

It was the love Abigail and Lucas held for one another that had created the idea of his matchmaking madness.

~~~~~~

Lucas held up the lantern to help guide his steps through the dark garden. He had torn through the manor in his search of Abigail. However, he hadn't found her in any of her usual hiding spots. He even searched the servants' quarters, but no one had seen her. Which only left the garden.

He hoped he found her soon, before she caught a chill. A wind had picked up, and a light caress of sprinkles fell on him. Abigail hadn't worn a shawl at dinner, and he knew she wouldn't have gathered one. She had wanted to disappear as quickly as possible.

"Abigail," he called out.

Nothing answered him but the rustling of the leaves on the trees and his shoes crunching on the loose gravel. His steps led him to the very destination where he had blundered his marriage proposal. He should've come here first because it was the very spot Abigail rested. She lay crumpled on the ground with her head on the bench. Shivers raked her body, and he thought they were from her grief. But as he drew closer, he realized Abigail had fallen asleep.

"Ah, love," he whispered.

He peeled off his suit coat and wrapped her in it, gathering her in his arms. He settled them on the bench and held her close to his heart, whispering comforting words. She never stirred in his arms except from the cold seeping into her, causing her body to shake. He carried her inside and to her room, where he laid her on the bed.

"Lucas," Abigail mumbled in her sleep.

"Shh, love."

He lifted the quilt over her sleeping form and stared down at her. Her hair spread out on the pillow and she snuggled into the warmth. He leaned over, brushing the hair from her face, and placed a soft kiss on her cheek. Lucas didn't have the heart to wake her, mostly in fear of the rejection sure to come his way. Also, he couldn't bear to see the heartache reflected in her eyes. Heartache he felt to the depth of his soul. Heartache he hoped to repair if she gave him the chance.

With a heavy heart, he left Abigail in peace and continued to his bedchamber. When he strode inside, he found Duncan sitting near the fire with a bottle of whiskey in his hand, ready for Lucas to drown his troubles in. Duncan held the bottle out, and he grabbed it before landing in the opposite chair. He took a long swallow of the fiery liquid. The heat sent fire to his belly, spreading out and warming his heart. The chill from watching Abigail in despair had taken up residence in his gut. It left him with wretched emotions he held no clue how to handle, much less express to Abigail.

"A bloody mess you have found yourself in this time," Duncan commented.

Lucas scoffed. "Thank you for your support."

Duncan laughed. "Anytime."

Lucas took another swallow. "How am I ever to repair the amount of pain I have caused Abigail?"

"With your love."

"The damage I have done far surpasses the emotion."

Duncan leaned forward with his hands folded between his knees.

"You underestimate the power of Abigail's ability of forgiveness and the love she holds for you."

"Perhaps I should leave for London tomorrow and give Abigail the space she needs."

Duncan grabbed the bottle away from Lucas. "No! You will not escape like a coward. You will stay and fight for Abigail. If you do not, then you will lose the most precious gift within your grasp."

Duncan rose, drinking from the bottle, and lunged over to Lucas, continuing his rant. "Over the past few years, I have listened to you whine and bemoan how unfair your life was when your father kept you betrothed to Selina. I even stood by your side when you left town right before your marriage ceremony."

"I left for your sake," Lucas interrupted.

"Bollocks. You left to save your own hide."

Lucas shrugged but offered no other excuse.

"Then you had every opportunity at your disposal to court Abigail. Yet you kept your distance, unless you felt the need to stake your territory of her person."

"Nonsense," Lucas muttered.

Duncan arched an eyebrow. "Oh, did you think your behavior when Lord Falcone visited didn't reach us? We heard in complete detail how you embarrassed Abigail at the bookstore by calling out Falcone."

Lucas scowled. "That reprobate touched her inappropriately."

Duncan fixed him with a stare. "He never did so. You were jealous of the time they spent together, walking in the gardens. Any gentleman who paid interest in Abigail, you scared off with your possessiveness. You don't want her for yourself, yet you want no other gentleman to win her affections. Well, my friend, the time has come for you to either love Abigail or to set her free. The family decided after you left the dining room that we will no longer run interference, nor will we stand in Abigail's way if she wants to leave."

"Abigail is not leaving."

"I am afraid that is no longer your concern. Tomorrow, your father will give Abigail her freedom. If you have any sense of decency, you will leave her alone if she accepts his offer."

Lucas shoved himself out of the chair. "One minute, you're spouting for me to seek Abigail's forgiveness. The next, you order me to leave her alone. Which is it?"

Duncan shrugged. "Which choice do you wish for? That is the decision you must make. But do not linger with your decision."

Duncan shoved the bottle back into Lucas's grip and walked out of the room, leaving Lucas alone with his thoughts. Thoughts that would turn any man insane, but ones Lucas already held the answers to. He only wished he had a plan to win Abigail's love.

Lucas stared at the bottle in his hand, knowing there were no clues hidden within. But the pity he held for himself led him to indulge his sorrows with the liquor at his disposal.

He drew his chair near the fireplace and propped his feet up on the other chair. With each drink he took, inspiration struck him on how he would apologize. By the time he finished the bottle, he had accumulated a list of ideas, each one more ridiculous than the last. However, he realized the only way to prove himself was to wear his heart on his sleeve and show Abigail how madly in love he was with her.

Lucas was ready to embrace the madness.

~~~~~

When Abigail awoke, she sensed she wasn't alone. Her friends filled her room, waiting for forgiveness. When she ran away from them the evening before, they had filled her heart with betrayal. However, once she calmed, she had realized they only had her best interest at heart. It didn't lessen the sorrow any, but it helped to ease her conflicting emotions. In their efforts to teach Lucas a lesson, their actions showed Abigail their loyalty. There were no truer friends than the ladies in this room. They were more than friends. They were her sisters.

"I forgive every one of you," Abigail told them. She opened her eyes and found them staring nervously at her.

Gemma smiled. "You may stay angry with us for a longer period."

Abigail sighed, sliding up to rest against the headboard. "I know, but 'tis not my nature. Also, I hope with the remorse you suffer from, you will promise to help me."

"Anything you ask we will make happen," Charlie swore.

"I wish to leave Colebourne Manor today."

"Where do you wish to go?" Jacqueline asked.

"To London for now. Tomorrow or the next day, who knows."

Selina handed Abigail a hot chocolate. "Duncan and I are traveling to London today. You may ride with us. Once we reach London, you are welcome to stay at our townhome."

Abigail shook her head. "I could not impose."

"Please," Selina pleaded. "I regret how I deceived you and I wish to make it up to you."

Abigail grabbed Selina's hand. "When I offered my forgiveness, it also included you. You are as much my sister as Gemma, Jacqueline, Charlie, and Evelyn are."

Selina sniffled. "A sister?"

Abigail nodded. "A sister."

"Then will you accept my offer?"

"Yes. Only you must promise we can leave immediately."

Selina squeezed Abigail's hand. "I will have Duncan ready the carriage."

After Selina left, a comforting silence filled the room. Abigail's gaze fell on the packed bags she had prepared to leave with Lord Ross. Now she embarked on a different journey. Only, she held no clue about the destination. However, she wasn't brave enough to face Lucas yet. She needed more time before she forgave him. Oh, she would eventually. She always did and always would. But the grief remained too fresh to deal with now.

"Do you have a plan?" Jacqueline asked.

"No. But I think I might give London a chance. I never explored the city last year because I was determined to believe I would never belong."

"But you always have," Evelyn protested.

Abigail held up her hand. "I understand that now. That is why I cannot remain upset with any of you. Your actions once again showed proof of the love you hold for me. Before, I made excuses about how I perceived my place in this family. Now I understand my value."

Charlie tilted her head and stared at Abigail. "And Lucas?"

Abigail swung her legs off the bed, pressing her hands into the mattress. Lucas. He was a subject she couldn't answer truthfully because each time she convinced herself there could be nothing between them, she remembered how the comfort his embrace made her feel. How the taste of his kiss sent her heart racing. How the whisper of her name against his lips set her soul on fire. How she found her home when she stared into his eyes. Loved and secured. Lucas was her best friend and the love of her life. Yet, she didn't much care for him at the moment.

She continued to rise and prepare for her departure. "A topic I do not wish to discuss."

"Are you giving up on him?" Charlie persisted.

"Leave her be," Jacqueline scolded her. Charlie crossed her arms and glared at her sister. Jacqueline shook her head and mouthed, "Not now."

Evelyn rose and helped Abigail dress. After Charlie finished pouting, she helped Abigail pack. She hugged each of them and gave one last longing glance at the bedroom Colebourne gifted her when she was lost and alone and had no one. But she had never really been alone. She always had a family and always would, no matter what decision she made.

"I love each of you," Abigail whispered.

She turned to leave, but Gemma's question stopped her. "Do you still love Lucas?"

Abigail looked over her shoulder, tears streaming down her cheeks. "I will until my last dying day and beyond."

Chapter Twenty

Abigail trailed around the parlor, picking up trinkets and setting them back down again. Memories from her time spent here filled her soul with heart-wrenching nostalgia. She curled into her favorite chair and stared out the window at the roses blossoming into an array of splendid colors. Pink, red, and yellow buds dotted the landscape, hoping to become the most breathtaking flower in the garden. She would miss the comfort she found here more than anywhere else.

Abigail tried to draw in the same hope for herself. Could she allow the hope to bloom in her heart? Or should she snip the bud before the thorns of life poked her again?

"I thought I might find you in here," Colebourne spoke from the doorway. Abigail started to rise, but Colebourne motioned for her to stay seated. "Do you mind the company of an old man?"

Abigail smiled. "I would love your company."

Colebourne chuckled. "I see you did not refute the claim of my age."

Abigail laughed. "I apologize, Your Grace, for not correcting you on your youthfulness."

Colebourne frowned. "Your Grace? I have made a mess of things with you after all."

Abigail patted his hand. "No. You have not."

Colebourne sighed, gripping her hand. "Ah, dear. I only ever wished the very best for you. When I took you under my wing after your mother passed, you stole my heart. I looked upon you as my daughter. Over the years, I watched the bond between Lucas and you intertwine. It reminded me of my marriage with Olivia. And in my selfish desire to see you two wed, I ruined the bond with my matchmaking mischief. Can you forgive an old man?"

Abigail's lips twitched at Colebourne poking fun of himself again. "Only if you can forgive a naïve girl for taking so long to accept the love of this family. I cannot find fault with your interference when I wished for the same outcome. Even when he was out of my grasp because of his betrothal, I never stopped wishing Lucas would declare his love for me."

"Do you still hope for your wish to come true?"

Abigail's smile twisted. "Some wishes are never meant to be."

"And the wishes that are?"

"Well, then the spirit of magic will sprinkle down upon them, helping their cause."

A twinkle appeared in Colebourne's eyes. "Magic and hope, that is all one can believe in."

Abigail never responded. She didn't wish to encourage Colebourne when she was unsure of herself. Abigail folded her hands in her lap. "I know you do not wish to hear my gratitude. But I will be forever thankful for the love and guidance you gave me over the years. You showed me how patience and forgiveness will heal any heartache one must endure. I've never expressed how much you mean to me, but I wish to now. I love you as a father. My mother never told me anything about my father, but over the years, I secretly imagined you as mine."

Colebourne folded his hands across his chest. "Then, as your father, may I ask what your plans are?"

"I plan to travel to London with the Forresters. Selina invited me to stay with them. I want to give the season another chance and explore the city as I should have done last year. While I am not comfortable in your world, I do not fit in with the servants, either. I need to find the place where I can be my best self. And to do that, I must give new opportunities a chance."

Colebourne rubbed his hands together. "I could not agree more. With your stay at the Forresters, Susanna can continue to act as your chaperone."

Abigail rose. "It is time for me to leave."

Colebourne rose and held out his arms. Abigail went into them and received her first hug from the man she considered a father. The comfort gave her the encouragement she needed to start afresh.

"Will you still join me for tea once in a while?" Colebourne asked.

Abigail winked. "I would not miss it for the world."

Colebourne reluctantly let Abigail go. He wanted to keep her at Colebourne Manor but understood the need to discover herself on her own terms. He only hoped it wasn't too late for his son.

Once she reached the door, he had to ask. "Is there anything you wish for me to tell Lucas?"

Abigail turned and her gaze traveled around the parlor, memorizing every detail. Once she landed on Colebourne, she shook her head. Just as she wouldn't give Colebourne any hope, she couldn't give Lucas any, either.

If one had no hope, then one wouldn't get disappointed with the outcome. Or would they?

~~~~~

Lucas staggered out of his bedchamber, searching for the source of the deafening ruckus. Servants were flittering in and out of his cousins' bedchambers, carrying luggage down the stairs. He stepped out of the way before a trunk swiped him.

Kincaid stepped into the hallway. "I will return after I check with Ralston on our departure."

Lucas called out before his friend reached the stairs. "Kincaid." Kincaid stopped and waited for Lucas. They started down the stairs together. "I thought you were staying on through the weekend."

"Everyone is making the journey to London earlier than planned. Please forgive me, but I cannot talk right now. I must find Ralston. Jacqueline is eager to start the journey, and we want to reach the halfway point by nightfall."

Lucas waved him off. "Of course, I understand. Is everyone leaving?"

"Yes," Kincaid called over his shoulder.

By everyone, did he also mean Abigail? No. She wouldn't leave. Would she?

Lucas rushed back upstairs, rounded the corner, and hurried to Abigail's bedchamber. Her door stood wide open and there was no activity inside the room. He took a tentative step inside, noting the emptiness.

She left.

There was no sign showing she remained. No bottles of perfume, hairbrush, or ribbons decorated the vanity. No books or candles rested on the nightstand. Even her shawl no longer took up residence on her rickety chair. While he slept off the whiskey, she had disappeared. He had lost his chance to beg for forgiveness.

"She left with Duncan and Selina early this morning," Evelyn spoke behind him.

"To Scotland?"

"Nay. To London. She wants to attempt the season again."

Lucas turned slowly, shocked by Evelyn's words. "You must be mistaken."

Evelyn shook her head. "I am not."

"Why?"

Evelyn shrugged. "Something you will have to ask her yourself."

"How? She made her decision quite clear when she left before giving me a chance to explain."

"Mmm. I never figured you for a quitter." Evelyn left and went to Jacqueline's bedroom.

Lucas followed and leaned his shoulder against the doorjamb. "Do I stand a chance?"

"You will never find out if you do not try," Evelyn stated.

A finger poked him in his back. Gemma stood behind him, rubbing her stomach. Lucas stepped to the side for her to enter and helped her into a chair.

"If he does not try what?" Gemma asked.

"To win Abigail's hand," Jacqueline answered.

Charlie tsked from the doorway. "That is quite a challenge for him to undertake." She looked him up and down. "Do you imagine he will succeed?"

Jacqueline winked at Lucas. "I believe he will."

"So do I," Evelyn added.

Gemma narrowed her gaze. "As long as he does not hurt her again, I say he should try."

Charlie linked her arm through Lucas's arm. "If he does, we will feed him to Selina. She has become quite descriptive with her ideas of torture since she married Duncan."

The girls laughed with delight, but Lucas cringed at the idea of enduring Selina's idea of torture. While Charlie only meant to lighten the mood, he understood her meaning. If Abigail suffered another moment of heartache from his hands, then they would make him suffer.

"I will make a solemn vow to each of you by promising to make sure Abigail feels loved every day for the rest of her life."

Jacqueline nodded with approval. "That is all we have ever wanted."

~~~~~~~

Lucas saw his cousins and their spouses off. He learned his grandfather, aunt, and uncle had left earlier with Duncan, Selina, and Abigail. Which only left his father and him remaining in the empty manor. His father never spoke his goodbyes and remained hidden away for most of the day. Lucas knew where he would find his father, and he wasn't mistaken.

The door to his mother's parlor stood open, and his father sat in his favorite chair, staring out the window. Lucas had only taken a few steps into the room when he breathed in Abigail's fragrance. She had told his father goodbye, but not him. His father looked over at him, and Lucas felt his father's sorrow. It was in that moment that he realized how deeply his father cared for Abigail. Oh, he knew he cared for her as his ward and treated her no differently than he did his cousins. But what Lucas hadn't taken into effect was how his father loved Abigail as a daughter.

Lucas walked to the bookcase and drew out a book of poems his mother favored. He sat across from his father and laid the book on his lap.

"She left," his father said. Lucas nodded. Colebourne cleared his throat. "I let her go to seek her freedom."

Lucas traced the lettering on the cover. "She will return."

"You sound confident."

Lucas looked his father square in the eye. "Because I am."

"I suppose you have your own plan."

Lucas scoffed. "I think you have interfered enough with yours."

Colebourne chuckled. "Perhaps a bit of advice?"

Lucas flipped open the book to the page earmarked. "And that would be?"

"Make a grand gesture," Colebourne suggested.

"Such as?"

"I will leave that detail for you to decide."

Lucas laughed. "Thank you."

Colebourne leaned back, resting his hands on his stomach. "I only ever wanted you to share the same happiness with Abigail that I shared with your mother."

Lucas nodded. "I know."

"Am I forgiven?"

"There is nothing to forgive. A father's love is only as strong as a child's love in return. I understand your actions. Even if they were a bit mad."

Colebourne chuckled. "Madness runs in the family."

"'Tis something to look forward to."

Colebourne pointed at the book. "Page forty-five?"

"I thought it would be appropriate."

"Yes, 'tis perfect."

Colebourne closed his eyes as Lucas read from the book. The poem was his mother's favorite that they shared with nobody else but each other. After his mother died, they had spent many hours together in this parlor grieving for the lady who had the most impact on their lives. Not a day passed by without them remembering the depth of her loss.

Lucas read until his father fell asleep. He set the book on the table and covered his father before returning to his room. While they never discussed their departure, Lucas knew his father wished to follow everyone soon. So he packed his bags, preparing for when they would leave for London. He would give Abigail a few days before he pursued her. Then he would give her what she deserved. A proper courtship with everyone in London watching how much he loved her.

He would leave no doubt in Abigail's heart of his intentions.

Chapter Twenty-One

"Another bouquet. You, my dear, are a success," Aunt Susanna gushed.

"Yes, your suitors are showering you with an abundance of flowery mementos," Selina quipped, rubbing the petals of the latest arrangement to arrive.

Abigail rolled her eyes at the displays. "They are truly in excess. Can we not donate them to the hospitals or churches?"

Susanna gasped. "That would be an affront. If any of the gentlemen learned of your ungratefulness, it will unravel any progress we have made."

Abigail sighed. She didn't care about the progress she had made or how she drew the infatuation of numerous gentlemen. She only cared about one gentleman in particular. One who had made himself scarce. Which was her fault because she hadn't spoken with him when he paid a visit after he arrived in town. She had avoided him, pleading a headache.

Everyone thought she remained furious with him, but she had actually forgiven Lucas before she arrived in London. After she mulled over his reasons for deceiving her, she understood why he had continued with the deceit. She had read the letters he wrote, impersonating Lord Ross, over again. As she read between the lines, she saw what she had missed before.

The letters were full of their intimate thoughts. They had shared their fears and dreams with one another, just like they used to when they were friends. Deep inside those letters, Abigail rediscovered the man she fell in love with all those years ago. While she tried to run away, he tried to keep her close.

Selina winked, pulling the card out of the latest bouquet. "'To the loveliest beauty who has ever graced London. Your appearance is as bright as the sun after a summer shower. Refreshing and intoxicating to the senses. Your secret admirer.'"

Abigail pretended indifference. The gentleman had yet to introduce himself, and his daily card with a flower arrangement left her wondering when they would meet. A footman or carrier never delivered them. Whoever left them on the stoop went unnoticed. Aunt Susanna thought her entrance into society was a hit, but Abigail feared her admirer would never present himself.

"Would you mind if we stayed in this evening?" Abigail asked.

Selina and Susanna passed a glance between each other. Neither of them wished to pressure Abigail into the entertainments. But they knew Lucas's plan to attend the Mitchel Musical this evening to pay court to Abigail. It was his way of apologizing for his behavior from last year's musical, where he forced Abigail into attending with his harsh words.

Abigail noticed the look the two ladies shared and felt guilty for ruining their attempts to bring her out into society. "Never mind. It is only the Mitchel Musical. I enjoyed it last year and I am sure I will find delight in attending again."

"If you are sure, dear. If not, I can send our excuses. Lady Mitchel will understand," Aunt Susanna reassured Abigail.

"Nonsense. She is your good friend and has shown her kindness by including me in the festivities. Also, Evelyn and Charlie mentioned they were to attend too."

"Then shall we choose your dress for the evening?" Selina asked.

Abigail smiled. "Lead the way."

Abigail followed Selina upstairs. After they arrived in London, Selina took Abigail to her modiste and they designed a different wardrobe for Abigail. Abigail never favored the demure colors of a debutante but admired the bold fabrics that highlighted her red hair. From the attention she received, the gentleman admired them on her too.

However, she only wished for one gentleman to admire them, but he stayed absent from any entertainment she attended. She refused to question his whereabouts. She didn't want to draw attention to her need to see him. It would only start everyone's interference all over again. Perhaps tomorrow she would visit Colebourne for tea, as she had promised him. Then, if she bumped into Lucas, her visit would be even more wonderful.

Abigail nodded at all the right times as Selina helped her prepare for their evening. She couldn't remember what her friend talked about because she was too busy planning her visit to Colebourne's townhome on the morrow. A smile settled over Abigail's face once she realized how she might see Lucas soon.

~~~~~

Lucas arrived at the musical late. He snuck into the back, his eyes adjusting to the darkness. A few candles were lit near the piano and the other musicians. He wanted to catch Abigail unaware, so she couldn't flee once she saw him. His gaze searched the chairs for any sign of her.

He found her sitting between Selina and Aunt Susanna. She wore her hair pulled into a twist upon her head, with a few strands dangling along her neck. He wished he sat next to her, where he could brush them aside and press his lips against her creamy skin. Her sighs would blend in with the music. His fingers itched to caress her. The past few days had been sheer torture with her so close but still so far out of his reach.

Is she still upset with me?

His entire family had informed him of the warm greeting Abigail had received at the functions they attended. He had yet to hear any whispers proving otherwise, but he knew how the gossip mill operated. They would try to hide any slanderous words until it was too late for Abigail to act otherwise. If anything, they found enjoyment from her to liven up any entertainment. He hoped that wasn't the case, which kept him on edge.

He paid no attention to the music, except for how the haunting melody echoed the longing in his soul. Lucas had never experienced such a sense of loss as he had since Abigail left. Even though he and his father had traveled to London a few days later, he felt adrift, lost in the inevitable destruction of his life without Abigail.

Abigail sensed the moment Lucas entered the musical. A ripple of awareness sent shivers tingling along her spine. She closed her eyes and let the melody invade her soul as she pictured the tips of Lucas's fingers whispering against her skin. His warm breath caressing her neck right before his lips placed the softest of kisses below her ear.

"Come with me," he whispered. Abigail imagined Lucas's unspoken plea.

But the need to be alone with him wiped away every rational thought she held. If she rose and he followed, then any misgivings she had about them she had to bury in the past. It would signal her forgiveness and show Lucas he could pursue her if he so chose. If she remained in her seat, then she would never discover his intentions. It would show Lucas how she would never forgive him and there wasn't any hope of a courtship between them.

"Please forgive me. I must use the ladies' room," Abigail whispered to Aunt Susanna.

Aunt Susanna patted Abigail's hand in acknowledgement. "Do not be too long," her chaperone whispered back.

Abigail nodded and slipped out of the room. She waited in the empty hallway for Lucas to join her. Once a door opened, she started walking along the hallway, heading deeper into the house. Soft footsteps followed behind her. She didn't need to turn to know it was Lucas.

Lucas followed Abigail, keeping a respectable distance between them in case anyone lingered in the shadows to catch them unaware. When she left the musical, he had grasped at the chance to redeem himself. Selina and his aunt had shared a wink between each other, a sign they wouldn't follow Abigail or search for her if she stayed away for any length of time. While his family promised not to interfere, he also knew they couldn't help themselves if an opportunity presented itself to offer their support.

Abigail stopped at an open door. Her head turned slightly to look over her shoulder, but she paused. Waiting. He didn't allow her another second of doubt and wrapped his arms around her waist and drew her inside the room. Lucas closed the door and pressed Abigail against the wooden panel. She melted in his arms and circled her hands around his neck.

Lucas groaned as she pressed her body into his. Every honorable intention he had diminished with her soft curves molding to his hard frame. He rested his forehead against hers, fighting the temptation she presented. He never imagined she would be so willing to fall into his embrace. Lucas thought he would have to coax a kiss from her lips. He was out of his element with the seductive siren in his arms.

"Kiss me," Abigail whispered.

"There is so much I need to say to you. I need to seek your forgiveness."

Abigail placed her finger against his lips. "Shh. No talking. No promises. No asking for forgiveness."

Abigail asked Lucas for the impossible with her request. He wouldn't understand how to react because of his need for control. He expected everyone to act properly. Lucas needed life explained before he ventured further. Abigail wanted Lucas to act spontaneous, wanted him to show her how they wouldn't keep their love hidden in a box. She needed him to throw caution and decorum to the wind and become so captivated with her that nothing or no one else mattered but her.

What Abigail wanted most of all was for passion to rule Lucas's actions.

Abigail's declaration of not asking for forgiveness almost stopped him from kissing her. But the desire blazing in her eyes clouded any decency he clung to. Her fingers glided through his hair, guiding him toward her mouth. Abigail's tongue darted out to wet her lips, and at that moment, he lost his ability to remain in control.

Lucas lowered his head and devoured Abigail's mouth. With every sweep of his lips, stroke of his tongue, and groan of his need for her, he let Abigail understand how she affected him. He lost himself when she sighed into their kiss. As they got lost in the passion, their love intertwined them into an unbreakable bond. He would profess the speech he had prepared later. Now he only wanted to get lost in Abigail's kisses. Each one was sweeter than the last.

Abigail clung to Lucas with a desperation she didn't realize she was capable of. While she had made herself a promise to accept wherever their love took them, she realized she had lied. She could never accept if Lucas turned his back on their love. She needed him more than she needed to breathe. Without him, life would remain an empty vessel, unfulfilled.

When his lips kissed a path of fire along her neck, Abigail pressed her body closer. She ached for him to caress her flesh. To have him dip his hand inside her dress and ease her sensitive buds. To have him draw them into his mouth and moan his pleasure.

"Oh, my. Please touch me," Abigail begged.

Lucas stared down at Abigail. The tempting sight of her undid him. Her lips were full and pouty from their kisses. Her gaze pleaded with him to fulfill her request.

"Here?" Lucas asked. His fingers trailed across the neckline of her dress that dipped low enough to tease him with the delights hidden inside.

Abigail whimpered at his touch.

"Or lower?" He teased her by sliding his fingers under the silken material and dipping between the valley of her breasts.

"Lower." Abigail's husky demand enflamed his senses.

His fingers dipped lower, brushing across a hardened nipple. When Abigail drew in a ragged breath, he slowly drifted across to the other nipple. His hand cupped her breasts as he gently twisted the bud between his fingers. Lucas glanced down and watched her nipples press against the fabric, straining for release. He bent his head and trailed his tongue in between her breasts.

"I cannot wait to suck your sweet buds between my lips again."

Abigail's whimpers increased. What Lucas desired was for her moans of pleasure echoing around them. But he would wait. He refused to draw scandal to Abigail's good name, no matter how much he wanted her. However, he needed her scent wrapped around him until he could make her his again.

He hitched her leg around his hip. Abigail's breathing grew more ragged. One more touch and then he would let her go.

"Nor can I wait for the day when my mouth captures your desires while you scream my name. For now, a touch will tide me over." Lucas teased his hand over Abigail's wetness. Her desire coated his fingers as he slid one inside her, and captured her moan with a kiss. He meant to stop with just one caress. But with each stroke, he lost himself to the passion that demanded its need fulfilled.

Abigail exploded around him, and he gathered her close, softly kissing her while she recovered. He was a scoundrel for seducing her. However, his gentlemanly intentions vanished at her first glance. While he had never apologized, his intention wasn't forgotten.

Abigail nestled in Lucas's embrace. She knew he fought with his conscience. Usually, guilt would overcome her for causing him distress, but all was fair in love and war. And until Lucas set all practical matters aside, then she would tempt him until the madness overtook him.

She embraced how deliciously wanton her behavior was. She, Abigail Cason, who walked the same line as Lucas Gray on proper decorum, had allowed herself a scandalous tryst. Now she understood why her friends had risked their reputations as they had. While she had always loved Lucas, it was a young girl's infatuation. Now, she risked a woman's heart for his love in return.

A soft knock sounded on the door, shocking Lucas into dropping his hold on Abigail and stepping away. Abigail wanted to giggle at his reaction. Instead, she regained her balance and smoothed out her dress. She straightened her neckline and patted her hair to make sure her coiffure remained in place. When she raised her head, Lucas was scowling at her breasts.

"Aunt Susanna allowed you out of the house in that dress? Your breasts are on full display for any gentleman to fantasize about," Lucas growled.

And once again, he turned into a proper bore. But a jealous one, so Abigail would allow his rant.

She patted his cheek, amused by his stiff behavior. "The style of my dress did not stop your roving hands."

"I . . . Ahh . . . That is . . ."

Before Lucas defended his actions, Duncan's whisper reached them through the panel. "Abigail, if you are alone with Lucas in there, you must leave."

"Bugger off," Lucas hissed.

"Why is it I am always rescuing the members of this family from scandal?" Duncan muttered.

"Because you wish them to remain untainted by gossip," Selina soothed him.

Abigail smiled at Selina's need to reassure Duncan that he acted out of respect for all of them. She opened the door a crack, and Selina raised her brows in question. Abigail winked at her friend.

Selina giggled and slid her arm through her husband's and drew him away. "We will wait down the hall. But please hurry, the musical is almost over."

Abigail nodded. She closed the door and stepped over to Lucas. She smoothed down his hair from their act of passion, slid her hands down his suit coat, and adjusted his cravat. Then she reopened the door. Before she left, she needed Lucas to understand her own desires.

"And I long for the day when each of your kisses and caresses makes me yours again."

With those parting words, Abigail sauntered down the hallway and joined Duncan and Selina, who escorted her outside of the doors that led into the musical. They each grabbed a glass of champagne and pretended they were deep in a conversation when the rest of the guests filed out of the musical. None of them were the wiser of her disappearance for a short but memorizing time with Lucas Gray. A marquess who left her speechless with the whisper of his kisses and his magical touch. A gentleman who captured her soul with his love.

Lucas gripped the doorknob, fighting against the new flood of desire racking his body. Abigail's parting words tempted him into striding out and claiming her with a possessive kiss. However, when his father mentioned a grand gesture, it wasn't one to bring scandal to her name. And his mindset at this moment was one of domination. He felt like a caged tiger at the restraint he must show to society.

Now, how was he to stroll amongst the guests and watch every gentleman undress Abigail with their eyes? What was his aunt thinking to allow her to leave in that dress? After he stood back to admire her attire, his body had had a mind of its own. He had wanted to press her against the wall and possess her in one thrust. No seduction, just pure animalistic need. What had he turned into? The love he once held for Abigail started as a simple act of friendship that slowly turned to love. Now he was a man whose love for a woman flowed through his veins with a need that would never find satisfaction. A love unlike anything he had ever known.

Lucas found a spot to seclude himself away as he watched a bevy of suitors surround Abigail. She smiled at them with polite interest, but her gaze kept straying toward him. No longer did she offer him a shy smile, but a teasing glint shone from her gaze. It wrapped him deeper under her spell. When a young pup placed a kiss on her gloved hand, he scowled his displeasure.

"I notice you admiring Abigail's gown. We visited my modiste and created a new wardrobe for her. I am sure you will find pleasure when you see her dressed in them," Selina commented.

Lucas snarled. "I should have known you were behind her dramatic makeover."

Selina laughed. "Dramatic makeover? Why, even your description is *dramatic*."

"There was no need to change her. She was perfect as she was."

Selina took a sip of champagne. "Ah, Lucas. I cannot lay claim to her transformation. That all lies with you."

Lucas's brows drew together. "How so?"

"The result of your relationship with Abigail caused her to awaken from her cocoon and evolve into an amazing butterfly. Look at her, and I mean really take her in. She has grown confident of her place in this family. She never would have awakened if you hadn't shown her your love," Selina explained.

"But I only showed her my selfishness and caused her misery."

Selina smiled at him. "But Abigail has the ability to see into the depths of someone to understand why they behave as they do. She is generous with her forgiveness and loves freely. When you stop blaming yourself and accept her unconditional love, then you will discover a world of happiness at your feet."

Lucas returned her smile. "Our marriage would have been miserable. But you make a fine friend."

"I agree. And you are not too bad yourself, except for when you hurt my friend."

Lucas nodded in understanding. "Are you happy with Duncan, even with all the scandal surrounding your marriage?"

"Yes. We wouldn't have chosen it any other way. Do you plan to set aside your stuffy behavior for the same happiness?"

Lucas winked. "Yes. But first I plan to offer Abigail a proper courtship. Then if you are favorable, I want to create a scandal, declaring my love at your ball next week."

Selina's expression brightened at his plans. "I am very favorable."

"Perfect."

"What do you have planned for the courtship?"

Lucas shook his head. "I refuse to divulge my plans to any of you. I will only ask if Abigail received my flowers?"

Selina frowned. "When did you send them?"

"Every day since I arrived in town. However, I always left them on the doorstep."

Selina gasped, covering her mouth. "You sent the ones with the sappy sentiments."

Lucas cringed. "Too over the top."

Selina laughed. "No. They are perfect, now that I realize who sent them."

Lucas frowned. "I had hoped she would recognize my manuscript."

"You still have much to learn." Selina patted his cheek before leaving.

Abigail watched Lucas's dumbfounded expression after talking with Selina. At one time, jealousy had consumed Abigail when she watched them together. Only because Selina and Lucas had been promised to one another and Lucas had been forever out of her reach. But now, she only found amusement at their inner action. Selina kept Lucas always questioning himself. Abigail couldn't have a better ally on her side.

When Lucas laid claim to her attention again, Abigail forgot about the other suitors vying for her attention and focused on him. When he raised his glass of champagne at her in a silent toast, Abigail's smile lifted in acknowledgement. He silently congratulated her on her success and she answered him with praise of his acceptance.

Chapter Twenty-Two

"If you showed any sort of patience, Lucas would have called on you today. We did not have to bother Colebourne with a visit," Selina informed Abigail, untying her bonnet.

"I am not calling on the duke to see Lucas. I promised Colebourne I would visit him for tea once he arrived in town. This is my first opportunity, and I refuse not to fulfill my promise," Abigail answered in defiance.

Selina hmphed. "Whatever you must tell yourself to convince yourself otherwise."

Before Abigail could defend herself, the butler, Goodwin, answered the door. "A pleasant surprise, Miss Cason and Lady Forrester. The duke will find joy with your arrival. He has waited for your visit."

Abigail smirked at Selina. "I hope we have not come at an inconvenient time."

"No. The duke and Lord Gray are reading in the library. Would you like to surprise them?" Goodwin winked.

"Please."

"I will inform the housekeeper to add two more cups for tea."

"I told you he expected me," Abigail gloated to her friend.

"Arrogance does not suit you, my friend." Selina tried to bite back a smile.

Abigail laughed. "I agree. I found pleasure from the duke waiting for my visit and allowed it to go to my head."

"Understandable, especially after you told me how he considers you a daughter."

Abigail and Selina paused at the doorway before announcing their presence. They watched Lucas pace back and forth before the fireplace, with Colebourne watching him in amusement.

"Do you think she will show today?" Lucas asked with impatience.

The duke caught sight of them and winked. He nodded his head to hide. Selina pulled Abigail to the side, pressing them against the wall.

"Why the sudden urgency to see Abigail? I thought you saw her at the Mitchel Musical last night. Your aunt wrote to me this morning, telling me how you couldn't take your eyes off Abigail."

"Nosy busybody," Lucas muttered.

Selina and Abigail covered their giggles.

"Did she look lovely?" Colebourne asked.

"Like a walking dream come true. There are no words descriptive enough to describe how breathtaking Abigail is."

Selina sighed. "Ahh, how romantic."

"Maybe luck will shine our way today with a visit from Abigail."

Lucas slumped into a chair. "Luck has never befriended me."

"Perhaps your luck has taken a turn," Abigail said softly from the entryway.

Lucas scrambled to his feet when she spoke. He bumped into a side table in his attempt to reach her, then rubbing his hip, almost knocked over a vase in his impatience. Selina laughed at him as she passed him to hug his father. He stopped before Abigail and took in her smile that brightened the room.

"Hello."

He swiped back a lock of hair that fell over his eyes. "Hello."

He endeared himself to her with his sheepish smile. "How are you today?"

Lucas gulped. "I am well. How are you?"

"Better now," Abigail whispered for only Lucas to hear.

Lucas's eyes widened. "Were you ill?"

Abigail smiled. "No. Only missing you."

"Oh." A goofy smile spread across his cheeks. "Oh!"

"Come closer, Abby, so I can give you a proper greeting," Colebourne ordered.

Abigail giggled at Lucas before moving on to greet Colebourne. She wanted to address him as Poppa but would wait until Lucas married her. Were her thoughts too presumptuous? Perhaps. However, Selina had mentioned she had grown arrogant of late.

"Ahh, you two lovely ladies are a sight for sore eyes," Colebourne complimented them as he helped them to sit on the settee.

"I hope you do not mind, but I told Goodwin I wanted to surprise you," Abigail explained.

Colebourne chuckled, glancing at his son. "Oh, you are a pleasant surprise to our afternoon. Are they not, Lucas?"

Lucas shook his head, clearing out his thoughts. Especially the ones too inappropriate for the present company. "I apologize. What are we discussing?"

"How nice it is of Abigail and Selina to join us for tea."

"Yes, most pleasant," Lucas agreed, walking over to sit next to Abigail on the settee. Abigail slid over to make room for Lucas, jostling Selina.

Selina rolled her eyes at Lucas. "I think I prefer to sit over here." She rose and chose a seat next to Colebourne.

"Did you enjoy the musical?" Lucas asked Abigail.

"Yes, it was very enjoyable."

"Lucas just told me how lovely you looked. And Susanna has sent word of your success. I am very proud of you, my dear."

Abigail nodded at his praise.

"You look lovely today, too," Lucas sputtered.

A warm blush spread across Abigail's cheeks at Lucas's attention. He only spoke to her, ignoring his father and Selina. However, when Abigail glanced over at them, they only smiled their pleasure at Lucas's smitten behavior.

"Thank you," Abigail said.

Goodwin entered, followed by more servants carrying trays with tea and cake. Another maid trailed after them with a vase of flowers and sat them in the middle of the table. Goodwin instructed the servants to serve the tea and cake, then he ushered them away.

Colebourne kept up the flow of conversation, filling the awkward silence with humorous stories of the time he courted Olivia. Throughout their visit, Lucas kept his gaze focused on Abigail. He would inquire of her activities in London, only to stop mid-sentence and stare at her. Selina and Colebourne kept making humorous remarks at his expense. However, Lucas remained clueless at their intent. After a while, they took pity and offered them a few moments of privacy.

"Selina, I have a letter for you to deliver to Susanna. Will you accompany me to my study?" Colebourne asked.

Selina winked at Abigail. "Yes. Then we must be on our way. Duncan has promised to take us for a ride through Hyde Park."

"A carriage ride through Hyde Park? That does not seem like Duncan's style," Lucas commented once Selina and his father left.

Abigail nodded. "Yes. Selina raves it is most fashionable for one to be seen riding in an open carriage."

"I was not aware you cared about being fashionable."

"I do not care."

Lucas frowned. "Then why agree to join them?"

"Because Selina is my friend, and she wishes to show me this pastime."

"Or does she wish for other suitors to claim your hand?" Lucas snarled.

This wasn't how she wished to spend her time alone with Lucas. To listen to his tone, she would think how the gentlemen paying her attention made him jealous. Which was absurd. Wasn't it? Abigail recalled other instances where gentlemen paid her attention, only for them to refuse to meet her eyes when they met again. Was Lucas the reason for their disinterest? She always thought he stopped other gentlemen from talking with her because he found them unsuitable to court her.

"I think it is time for me to leave. Your opinion of Selina is unfair. Especially with the loyalty she has shown you, even after the way you treated her." Abigail stalked toward the door.

Lucas caught her wrist and swung her around before she went very far. "Don't leave. Forgive me. The feelings I hold for you have turned me into a ranting lunatic. I have allowed my insecurities to surface, blaming others for my actions."

Abigail softened at his apology. She never meant to make him jealous. She only wanted to share another activity she would get to partake in. Since she had refused to enjoy them last season, she now embraced them and wanted to share them with Lucas.

"Will you join us?" Abigail asked.

Lucas wished for nothing more than to join them. But his jealousy would flare out of control, and he didn't want to ruin the outing for Abigail. "I cannot."

Abigail frowned. "Oh. All right. I hope you have a pleasant afternoon."

Lucas drew her into his arms when he heard the disappointment in her voice and brushed a stray curl behind her ear. "Not that I do not wish to, but I have an appointment scheduled with my solicitor I cannot miss."

Abigail relaxed in Lucas's arms once she realized he wasn't trying to avoid her. "Of course."

"Can I call on you tomorrow? I would like to escort you to a flower exhibit Lord Daborne is holding in his conservatory."

"I would enjoy that." Abigail gazed into Lucas's eyes.

Lucas lost himself in her adoring gaze. The golden flecks made the green in her eyes explode with color. He bent his head and drew her lips under his in a soft, slow kiss. Time stood still as he tasted the burst of lemon on her tongue. The tart flavor contradicted the sweetness of their kiss.

Abigail felt as if her feet lifted off the floor and she floated on a cloud. Lucas's kiss was gentle, yet he held his passion under tight control. A passion she wished to ignite but she knew they couldn't. But it didn't mean she couldn't tease him a little into unleashing himself a bit.

She traced her tongue around his lips, dipping inside to dance against his tongue, only to pull away. Lucas groaned and Abigail teased him again. Only this time, he tightened his embrace and his tongue stroked hers in a provocative dance of seduction, each stroke growing bolder than the one before. Abigail's moan reflected her need.

Lucas pulled away, dragging in deep breaths to calm his libido. "You make me forget myself."

Abigail skimmed her thumb across his lips. "'Tis my intention."

Abigail leaned forward and brushed her mouth against his. Then she winked at him as she drew out of his embrace. She joined Selina, who stood staring at them with an expression between shock and amusement. Lucas understood Selina's reaction oh so well. This new flirtatious side of Abigail shocked him, but he found immense pleasure with the vixen she portrayed.

His curiosity piqued to learn what else she held in store for him.

Chapter Twenty-Three

The next day, Lucas waited with impatience in the foyer for Abigail. He had declined to wait in the parlor when the Forresters' butler informed him she would be along soon. He wanted to watch her glide down the stairs in one of her new creations. After staring at her during tea yesterday, he admired how the new gowns hugged her form and displayed her womanly attributes. While he didn't care for any other gentleman gazing upon her, he wouldn't deny how they enhanced her beauty, showcasing her newfound confidence.

He heard footsteps and hurried to the stairs with a welcoming smile. However, when his uncle came into view instead, he grew disappointed. With a frown, he stepped back and took up his stance against the wall.

Ramsay cackled. "Not who ye were expecting?"

"Nay."

"If I were to slip on me kilt, could I tempt ye then?" Ramsay waggled his eyebrows.

Lucas bit back a smile at his uncle's quirky humor. "You are not quite my type."

"I have the same shade of hair."

Lucas nodded. "That you do. But still not my type."

"Ahh. I understand. Me kisses cannot compare to the lass's kisses," Ramsay answered with a devilish smirk.

Lucas laughed. "No, they would not."

Ramsay walked past Lucas, snickering his delight, and threw open the door. He peered outside and nodded his approval. "Plenty of room."

Lucas frowned. "For what, exactly?"

"For me and the missus to join your visit to the conservatory."

Lucas shook his head. "Oh, no."

Ramsay nodded. "Oh, yes."

Lucas continued shaking his head in denial. If his aunt and uncle joined them this afternoon, then he wouldn't get to have an openhearted conversation with Abigail. As much as she kept him from apologizing, they must talk, so they could move forward. While he enjoyed the flirtatious game they carried on, he wanted more. He needed to explain his deceit and declare his love to her.

"No!" Lucas tried one last time.

"No, what?" Aunt Susanna spoke from behind them.

"The boy was just telling me we cannot j—"

Lucas glared at his uncle, unhappy with how Ramsay was forcing his hand to accept their company. "I only told Uncle Ramsay that we cannot leave you ladies at the conservatory on your own and wait for you at our club playing cards. 'Tis not the act of a gentleman."

Susanna bussed his cheek. "I can always rely on you to keep the gentlemen in this family in line. You are so dependable."

Lucas smirked at Ramsay. "I only try to ensure your happiness."

Susanna glared at her husband. "Perhaps your nephew can teach you a few lessons."

Ramsay scoffed. "Lessons. I'll teach the boy a few lessons," he muttered after Susanna wandered over to the stairs.

Susanna turned. "I will check on Abigail. You gentlemen can wait in the carriage. We will join you shortly."

The gentlemen followed Aunt Susanna's instructions. However, after Lucas sat down, Ramsay sat next to him. He frowned and moved over to the opposite seat, only for his uncle to follow.

"Do you not wish to sit next to your wife?" Lucas asked.

"I would have, if you had not thrown me into the fire," Ramsay growled.

"You were about to tarnish my actions."

Ramsay shrugged. "I only tried to help you."

"By informing Aunt Susanna I didn't wish for you to tag along on my outing with Abigail?"

Ramsay sighed. "No. By making you see reason. Abigail cannot be seen without a chaperone, no matter what her status is in this family. She is still an unwed ward of your father's. There is already speculation surrounding her standing in society. If you would see reason, ye will realize I am here to steal my wife away for you to have time with Abigail alone."

Lucas closed his eyes once he realized how he had reacted first without seeing the full picture. "Oh."

Ramsay folded his arms across his chest. "Exactly."

Lucas noticed the ladies walking down the sidewalk toward the carriage and tried to bargain with his uncle. "What do you require of me to convince you to sit in the opposite seat?"

Ramsay twisted his lips, taking his time to contemplate his answer. "Anything?"

Lucas watched the ladies drawing nearer. A few more steps and they would reach the footmen waiting to assist them inside. "Anything."

Ramsay listed off his bribe. "A box of your father's finest cigars, a bottle of his rarest whiskey, and two dozen of your cook's chocolate biscuits."

Lucas narrowed his gaze, and Ramsay answered him with a quirk of his eyebrow. He glanced back out the window and saw the footman assisting his aunt up the step. "Fine," he growled.

Ramsay chuckled, moving across from him. "Ah, it is always a pleasure negotiating with you and your father."

"Swindling Scot," Lucas muttered under his breath.

"Pushover Englishman."

Susanna stepped inside the carriage, noting how her husband and Lucas sat on opposite benches. While one wore a scowl, the other wore a mischievous grin. Ramsay's smile only meant one thing. He had been up to his usual antics of causing trouble, and poor Lucas was the latest victim.

"Are you irritating my nephew?" Susanna whispered in Ramsay's ear.

"No, my love. Only negotiating."

"Mmm."

Abigail stepped into the carriage, and Lucas's frown disappeared. He reached for Abigail's hand and assisted her onto the bench. She smiled at him in gratitude. Whatever had disturbed Lucas no longer bothered him at the sight of the red-haired beauty. Susanna admired the couple from across the carriage. She found happiness that they had overcome their differences. They made a stunning sight and would have the most remarkable babies. Her brother-in-law would reprimand her for jinxing their union with the mere mention of babies, but Susanna couldn't help herself. The entire family waited on pins and needles for them to announce their engagement.

"Thank you for suggesting this outing, Lucas," Susanna said.

Lucas smiled. "My pleasure."

"I promised Lady Mitchel I would visit the exhibit. Her prized chrysanthemum is on display. At her musical the other evening, she bragged about the compliments she has received on the flower."

"Yes. She mentioned to me the unique color. I cannot wait to see it," Abigail added.

When he suggested the outing to Abigail, it had been his intention to find a spot for them to be alone. Now, with Susanna and Ramsay chaperoning, his plans were in shambles. He didn't find fault with his aunt for ruining his agenda when she only held Abigail's best interest at heart. However, he didn't enjoy his uncle smirking at him across the carriage.

Abigail kept offering him smiles in between her conversation with his aunt, and he soon forgot his irritation with his uncle. If she kept up her adoration, he would double his uncle's request.

"Thank you for inviting me today," Abigail whispered.

Lucas glanced across the carriage to see his relatives were deep in their own conversation. He focused on Abigail, taking in the warm blush across her cheeks. "It is my pleasure." Lucas's voice deepened.

Abigail twisted her hands in her lap, suddenly nervous at Lucas's bold stare. She glanced at the Forresters and saw they paid them no mind. They were too caught up with one another. "I am sorry for the additional guests."

Lucas traced his finger along the side of her gloved hand. "It is for the best."

Warmth flooded Abigail at his slight touch. "Oh. Why is that?" She raised her head, her gaze locking with his.

He leaned close, whispering only for her ears to hear. "Because if they did not join us, my actions would destroy every honorable code I hold. And for you to understand clearly, so you don't have to wonder, I would devour your sweet lips while my hands slid up your skirts and stroked your desire to a height where you would only find satisfaction from my touch alone. We would never have made it to the flower exhibit."

Abigail's pink blush soon turned to a dark red. Her eyes widened at his bold statement. She gulped, unable to form a coherent thought. She looked away, too flustered to meet his eyes. If she did, she couldn't hold back from what she most desired. Heaven forbid if she acted on her impulses. Her scandalous thoughts would cause the occupants of the carriage a shock they would never recover from.

Thankfully, their arrival saved her from any awkward moments. The carriage pulled to a stop at Lord Daborne's home. Since a line of carriages waited to disembark, the gentlemen exited first to help the ladies to the ground. Ramsay assisted Susanna, and they walked away, not even waiting for Lucas and Abigail to join them. When Lucas helped Abigail down, his hands lingered on her waist and he only pulled away with reluctance.

His attentions ruffled Abigail's composure. She tried to hurry after the Forresters, but Lucas pulled her behind some columns, blocking them from the other guests' view.

"I believe they are allowing us some time to ourselves," Lucas whispered in her ear.

Abigail stood on her tiptoes to look over Lucas's shoulder, but she lost sight of the Forresters in the crowd. She didn't know what to think of their abandonment. Nor did she understand her newfound nervousness with Lucas. The past few days, she had felt a boldness toward him with her wanton flirtation. Now she was once again sweet Abigail, unsure of where they stood. She didn't understand what had shifted. Perhaps it was how his gaze undressed her, the confidence in his swagger, and the deep undertone when he seduced her with his comments.

Lucas watched indecision cloud Abigail's gaze. No longer was she the tempting minx telling him of her desires and seducing him with the sway of her hips in her alluring clothing. Instead, she stood before him, indecisive about being alone with him. He took in her dress and noticed she once again wore the modest clothing she had before she arrived in London. *Why does she change the style of her clothing again?*

He stepped back from her a respectable distance, so as not to draw attention to them. "What has troubled you?"

Abigail frowned. "Nothing."

"May I ask a question regarding your attire?"

Abigail glanced at her dress, smoothing her hand along the skirt. "Is it not respectable enough? I am not embarrassing you, am I?"

Lucas appeared offended. "I have never held embarrassment over you. I only wish to ask, why you are not wearing one of your new dresses?"

Abigail folded her hands in front of her. "Because you appear to dislike them and I did not want to cause any whispers about my attire."

His foolish display of jealousy had caused Abigail to doubt herself. When would he ever learn how much of an impact his opinion had on her? Even if the thought of another man admiring Abigail drove him insane. He never meant to make her feel inadequate. He needed to reassure her otherwise.

Lucas tugged Abigail's hand, leading her deeper in between the columns. Once he felt they were secure enough away from any prying eyes, he drew her into his embrace. "My love. I never meant for you to doubt yourself. My bloody jealousy of the attention garnered your way drove me mad. You must wear whatever you desire. I adore you in rags and hold pride when you dress like a church matron. You hold my admiration when you dress to the hilt. But most important of all, I desire you in anything you drape across your luscious curves."

"Even if every gentleman strives for my attention?"

"Most especially if you are the belle of the ball. Because in the end, I know I am the one who holds your heart. Do I not?"

Abigail nodded. She wrapped her hands behind his neck and pulled his head down to hers. "You do," she whispered before kissing him.

Lucas moaned, falling under her spell. There was so much he needed to say to her, but every time their lips met, she entranced him, making him forget himself. He swung Abigail around and pressed her into the column. His desire ruled his every action. He pressed his hard cock into her core, enlightening a heavenly moan from her lips.

"Will you steal away with me tonight after everyone is in bed?" Lucas asked.

Abigail bit her bottom lip, unsure of his request. She wrestled with her conscience on the proper decorum she should display while a guest with the Forresters. But if she refused his request, she would miss out on an adventure. She no longer wanted to watch happiness surround her from afar. She wanted the whirlwind of life to catch her and embrace her with its unpredictability.

"Yes."

Lucas released a breath he didn't realize he held and swung Abigail in a circle in joy at her answer. He would make it a night for her to remember.

Abigail threw back her head and laughed, holding onto Lucas's shoulder. "You must put me down before I pass out."

Lucas slid Abigail along his body and pressed his forehead against hers. "Tonight," he whispered.

"Tonight," Abigail promised.

Lucas smiled, drawing Abigail's arm through his. He slipped them amongst the crowd, with no one catching them alone. They spent the afternoon admiring the blooming flowers. Once they caught up with the Forresters, they agreed that Lady Mitchel's flower was, in fact, quite spectacular. Lucas then treated them to flavored ices in Mayfair. It was quite an amazing afternoon.

Lucas thought his aunt and uncle would become a hindrance. Instead, they made themselves scarce as promised. Also, he had secured himself an interlude with Abigail for later this evening.

Today was a promising day. Hopefully, this evening would hold the same promise.

Chapter Twenty-Four

Abigail never thought to ask Lucas where she was to meet him after everyone settled in bed. She secured the belt of the long coat she wore around her waist. She hoped she didn't run into anyone, because if caught, she would never recover from the scandal.

When Lucas spoke of how her attire enflamed his desire, she wanted to entice him with the silky negligee she wore underneath her coat. Selina had dared her to purchase the scandalous nightgown. Once Abigail held the soft fabric between her fingers, illicit had thoughts floated in her mind and she accepted the dare. Now she waited with eagerness to see Lucas's reaction.

She jumped at a branch slapping against the side of the house. She hadn't realized the wind had increased. Abigail picked up the candle and wandered closer to the window to look outside. However, it wasn't a branch hitting the window, but little pebbles. Abigail looked out the window and saw Lucas tossing one pebble after another at her window. She blew out the candle and slid open the window.

"Lucas," Abigail whispered.

"Abigail." He dropped the pebbles and wiped his hands down his pants.

"Are you responsible for all this ruckus?" Duncan called out from his window.

Abigail gasped and pressed against the wall, mortified that Duncan had discovered Lucas.

"Quiet before your parents awaken," Lucas hissed.

Duncan scoffed. "As if they could sleep through all the commotion you are making."

"They will if you close your window and cease with all your ramblings."

Duncan leaned out the window. "Yer plan to steal Abigail away for a tryst wasn't planned out quite well."

Lucas swiped his hand down his face. "I realize that now."

"Perhaps you should have climbed the trellis near her balcony. Or at least snuck in through the library doors. You know my father never had the lock fixed."

Lucas closed his eyes and counted to ten, trying to rein in his irritation. If his cousin didn't stop blabbering, his aunt and uncle would soon learn of his arrival. Then the evening he had arranged for Abigail would be ruined.

"Shall we put Lucas out of his misery?" Selina whispered from the doorway.

Too caught up in listening to the gentlemen, Abigail didn't hear Selina enter. Now Selina was a witness to Abigail's embarrassment at getting caught sneaking out in the middle of the night. How had everyone else snuck out without ever getting caught?

Selina held her hand out in invitation. "If you do not leave now, you will miss your chance."

Abigail stepped out of the darkness, ran across the bedchamber, and took Selina's hand. Selina guided Abigail down the back staircase and to the door, which would lead her to Lucas. The turning point of her life. She rested her hand over her chest, hoping it would help settle the rapid beating of her heart.

Selina held Abigail by the shoulders, taking in her attire. A mischievous grin lit her face when she noticed Abigail's bare legs. "Are you wearing what I think you are?"

Abigail nodded.

"Oh, he does not stand a chance." Selina chuckled and urged Abigail to the door. "Go rescue your prince."

Abigail gripped Selina's hand before she left. "Thank you."

"Gratitude is unnecessary between friends. Only ensuring their happiness is." Selina smiled, then nodded for Abigail to go.

Abigail stepped outside and waited for Lucas to catch sight of her. Every wish she held was about to come true this evening.

Out of the corner of his eye, Lucas caught a slip of white moving from the townhome. He turned, and Abigail walked out of the shadows. His cousin's smart remarks no longer held his attention. Everything else faded away. Abigail's arrival was a beacon of light that overshadowed everything.

The memory of Abigail standing amongst the flowers with the breeze blowing her hair around would forever hold a place in his heart. It was the moment he understood what she risked by stealing away with him. He didn't need for her to express her affections with words; her actions alone spoke of the love she held for him. And he hoped she understood his love by his actions this evening and by the one he had planned for the night of Duncan and Selina's ball.

He strode over to Abigail and swept her into his arms. "You take my breath away."

Abigail curved her hand around his cheek. "As you do mine."

Duncan broke the spell that wrapped around them. "Daylight will break soon."

Lucas scowled at his displeasure. "Blabbering Scot."

Duncan's laughter spilled across the garden, sure to awaken the household. "No-nonsense Englishman."

Abigail's giggle drifted back to the window as Lucas whisked her away to the carriage.

Selina coaxed Duncan away from the window. "Leave your cousin be, my love. Your wife is in need of your attention."

Duncan strode to his wife's side, pulled her into his embrace, and ravished her lips. After a while, he lifted his head and whispered, "Is this sufficient? Or perhaps you desire more attention."

"Oh, definitely more." Selina's husky whisper spoke of the desires she wished for Duncan to fulfill.

In another wing, Susanna stood in awe of the couple in the garden. Her nephew held the ability to make a scandalous gesture, after all.

Ramsay urged Susanna away. "Come from the window, my dear. Allow the couple their privacy. You can gloat to Colebourne on the morrow of the miraculous event."

Susanna crawled into bed. "It is so romantic."

Ramsay rolled above her. "Do you wish for romance, my dear?"

Ramsay never allowed Susanna to answer. He took her lips in a sweet, endearing kiss. However, if she were to answer, it would be to tell her husband he filled every day of their marriage with romance.

~~~~~~

Abigail never left Lucas's arms. He set her on his lap for the entire carriage ride. When she asked about their destination, he told her it was a surprise, then spent the rest of the drive kissing her. In between his kisses, he whispered compliments of her beauty. Every time she attempted to respond, his mouth lowered, and she was at the mercy of his love. Each kiss was sweeter than the last.

Lucas fought to keep his passion reined in. Abigail's softness molded against him, letting him know she wore little under her coat. His fingers itched to peel the garment apart and discover what she wore. But he fought the temptation, knowing full well once they reached the cottage, he would unwrap her. Her kisses were a distraction enough to keep his thoughts at bay. While he kept them light, he sampled the passion they both craved to explore.

When the carriage stopped, relief overcame him. He no longer had to resist Abigail. Lucas disembarked with Abigail still in his arms, and his long strides covered the distance to the cottage. His coachman already had his instructions for the evening and would return for them before dawn. He had called in a favor, and when he glanced through the window, he noticed Ralston had fulfilled the requests as he asked.

The only item remaining was the most nerve-racking for him. The other details to set the scene were simple to accomplish. Laying himself open to Abigail and showing her every vulnerable side, however, was a daunting task he needed to fulfill.

When he stepped through the doorway, the atmosphere transported them into a romantic setting of seduction. Candles littered every available surface, bathing the cottage in their warm glow. Rose petals lined a path toward the fire that flickered in the hearth. Scattered across the floor were pillows and blankets, beckoning them closer.

Lucas set Abigail on her feet and stood back from her as she took in what he had prepared. "Would you like a glass of wine?"

Abigail trailed away, following the rose petals. Lucas had put forth a tremendous effort to seduce her this evening. However, Abigail didn't view it as a seduction. They both knew what he had implied when he asked her to steal away with him this evening. She agreed because she ached to have their connection wrap her in its warm embrace again.

Their brief visits and his anonymous flowers weren't the same. Oh, she had guessed who sent them on the first day but pretended ignorance when Selina poked fun of them. Abigail found them endearing and had slipped the cards into her pocket when no one watched. She then stored them with his other letters where he pretended to be Lord Ross. While she waited for Lucas to arrive, she had read through all the letters again. Every act declaring his love was stated. She had been too blind to see his intentions before. But no longer.

She turned around to face him. Lucas waited, unsure of her reaction. He stood still, afraid any movement would cause her to flee. The poor dear. He had suffered enough for his deceit. She untied the belt around her waist. Abigail no longer wanted their past to affect their future. She had forgiven him.

She opened the coat and slid it off, and it pooled around her feet. Abigail chose to love Lucas.

His groan filled the cottage at the sight of the thin garment molded to Abigail's curves. The negligee left nothing to the imagination. It only inflamed his desire to claim her again. The silk hugged her breasts and dipped low. One long slit opened the front of the decadent gown, tempting him to come closer. He needed no other encouragement to sweep the garment away and feast on her heavenly body.

Lucas strode toward Abigail with purpose. The gleam in his eyes informed her of his intentions. He didn't allow a single doubt to enter her mind when he grabbed her and drew her to the floor. His lips devoured her with a drugging effect of pure ecstasy.

"You, my dear, are a vixen set out to destroy my soul," Lucas whispered as his lips trailed a line of fire to her breasts.

"'Tis was my intent," Abigail whispered, arching her back. She ached for his lips to satisfy her needs.

Lucas's tongue licked along the valley of her breasts. The singe only intensified the need for the full burn. When his lips clamped onto her nipple through the lace, Abigail dug her fingers into his hair and held him close. He aroused her with soft licks and bites, while his hand slid up to where her gown opened and teased her with gentle caresses between her thighs. She opened her legs in welcome, but his fingers only brushed across her curls, never once touching where she most desired.

Abigail hitched her leg around Lucas's waist, opening herself to his touch. Her hands grew frantic and tore at his clothing. He chuckled and stood up, discarding his clothes, one piece at a time, in agonizing slowness. Abigail slid the straps off her shoulders, but Lucas shook his head at her to stop. Abigail obeyed, her straps forgotten when Lucas removed his pants. His desire pulsed between his legs.

Abigail rose to her knees, her hands guiding their way along his legs before curving around his muscular thighs. Her hand wrapped around his hardness and guided it between her lips. Gentle. Slow. Her tongue teased him with erotic strokes.

Lucas's breath hitched as he watched the goddess below him on her knees, pleasuring him. His legs almost gave out on him as her mouth wrapped around his cock. Her gown had slipped and her globes beckoned him in the firelight. The fabric clung just above her nipples, teasing him with a glimpse each time she shifted. When her mouth glided down his cock, drawing him deeper, he knew he would never last if he didn't stop her soon.

When Lucas tightened his hands in her hair, Abigail understood the power of her touch. Her tongue swirled around, chasing the pulsing of his hardness. With each beat, she pressed her mouth tighter around him. He arched his hips to match her movements, unraveling with each thrust.

When Abigail's fingers dug into his buttocks to take him in deeper, Lucas exploded. He couldn't control himself even if he tried. He was powerless to resist her sweet lips and the caress of her fingers. Abigail pulled away from him with victory in her gaze, and he lost himself in the passion surrounding them.

With a growl, Lucas lowered Abigail to the blankets and devoured her lips like a drunken man thirsty for one more drop of her sweetness. Except he couldn't quench his thirst. The taste of Abigail only made him thirsty for more. He rose above her and raked her form with his gaze, unsatisfied with how she remained covered. He wanted nothing more than to tear the gown off her and stake his claim. But as his eyes traveled back up her legs, he noticed the gown had risen around her hips, offering him a view of how wet Abigail was.

Abigail watched Lucas lick his lips as his eyes devoured her. If she thought he would ease her ache soon, she would be mistaken. Instead, he lowered her gown slowly where the whisper of soft silk caressed her skin as gently as he would soon.

The soft brush of his lips started at her ankles and climbed higher, applying more pressure. By the time his mouth hovered over her core, Lucas had heightened Abigail's senses to a need out of her control. Her body shook with desire, where only Lucas could ease the ache consuming her soul. His warm breath stroked the fire of her need.

With one soft caress of his tongue, Lucas eased the ache his body kept tightly strung. At his first lick, he savored Abigail's wetness. He ran his tongue around his lips and moaned at the exquisite flavor. Abigail's thighs shook around him with the barely controlled need she clung to. A need Lucas wanted her to relinquish to under his tongue.

He slid two fingers into her tight pussy and she arched higher, pressing her core against his mouth. He met her unspoken demands with each twist of his fingers and each lap of his tongue. When his tongue struck relentlessly against her clit, Abigail exploded around him.

"Lucas. Lucas," Abigail cried out.

Still, his satisfaction remained beyond his reach, waiting for her to unravel around him and offer him the same power he had given her. His tongue slowly stroked along her folds, his thumb brushing across her clit with a gentleness he far from felt. His mouth soothed her with kisses until she melted underneath him with soft moans, declaring her pleasure.

When she relaxed her hold against him, he started the sweet torture all over again. The stroke of his tongue grew firmer, his thumb pressed harder against her nub, and his mouth grew possessive, stealing every last will she held onto. He drew out her passion, building her need higher. When he had her right where he wanted her, hanging and ready to fly over the edge, he rose above Abigail and slid deep inside.

Abigail gasped at the powerful thrust of Lucas. She had been on the verge of breaking into a million pieces when he entered her and filled her completely. He paused deep inside and stared into her eyes. Abigail moaned at the intense emotion pouring from him and wrapping her into his embrace.

He leaned down and kissed her softly. His hand slid along her cheek and Abigail noticed how it shook against her. "I love you with everything I am, Abigail Cason."

Abigail slid her hand against his cheek. "And I love you with everything I am, Lucas Gray."

The love shining from Abigail's eyes wrapped around Lucas. He brought their hands together above Abigail's head and slid in and out of her slowly. Each movement rippled through them. Their gazes stay connected as they loved each other. Each moan echoing in the cottage played a melody their bodies ached to hear. When Abigail tightened around him, Lucas gave himself over to the power of their love.

Lucas rolled over and gathered Abigail close. He needed to bare his heart to her. However, it could wait. For now, he only wanted to enjoy the pleasure of holding Abigail in his arms.

Abigail nestled closer, soaking up Lucas's warmth. She wanted to assure him of her love. However, it could wait. For now, she only wanted to enjoy the pleasure of his arms wrapping her in his love.

In these moments, no words were necessary.

Chapter Twenty-Five

An arm flung across Lucas's chest before a leg kicked him in the side. He jerked awake, ready to protect Abigail, when he realized she was the one who had caused him harm. Still deep asleep, Abigail muttered incoherent words before wrapping her arms around a pillow and settling once again. Lucas chuckled, realizing the lifetime he would have to endure her restlessness.

He leaned over and trailed kisses along her neck. "Abigail, love. You must awaken soon."

Abigail moaned. "Mmm."

His mouth moved lower, lingering between her shoulder blades. "Or we can spend the entire day hidden away where no one can find us."

Abigail rolled over. "Are you trying to involve my good name in a scandal, Lord Gray?"

Lucas stilled until he saw the teasing glint in Abigail's eyes. "Never, my love."

Abigail shrugged. "That is a shame. My entry into society this year has been quite a bore since Selina and I are friends. I am treated no different than I was last season."

He brushed her hair from her eyes. "That is because everyone accepts you as my father's ward and my entire family will not stand for you to become a victim of the ton. They stand in defense of any untoward action."

She arched her brow. "And how do you stand?"

"As a proud gentleman who has won the honor of your love."

She cupped his cheek. "Was it too difficult?"

He sighed. "No. It is a simple act because of the love I hold for you."

Abigail frowned. "Then why all the deceit? Why did you keep me at arm's length after Selina wed Duncan? You still refused to accept the bond between us."

Lucas pressed his forehead against Abigail's. "I was a fool. I thought I had to follow the structures society demanded for the peers of the ton, even after witnessing each of my cousins defy those very structures to find happiness. I still refused to acknowledge I could define my own life. My father never allowed another soul to rule his actions. But yet I did."

"Do you still?"

Lucas cupped Abigail's cheek. "No. I stopped when I started writing to you as Lord Ross. I never expected our correspondence to last as long as it did. But with each letter, we drew closer and the feelings it invoked had me acting foolish once again."

"You had me accepting a position in your imaginary household."

Lucas winced. "I planned to confess before we left for London. However, by then, my father started with his game and my cousins got involved too. It caused a disaster I didn't know how to recover from. The confession I planned got fumbled with my disastrous marriage proposal. Can you ever forgive me for the heartache I have caused you this past year?"

Abigail pressed a kiss against Lucas's lips. "There is nothing to forgive. Both of us needed to grow before we could have our time together. I lived these past few years believing I never belonged, when your family had welcomed me since my first day at Colebourne Manor. I always kept myself separate because I tried to live by those same rules of society you yourself lived by. When all along, I only needed to be myself."

Lucas brushed her hair behind her ear. "And have you discovered yourself?"

"Yes, and I have you to thank for my transformation. You helped to free me from my doubts and become who I wish to be."

"And who do you wish to be?" Lucas whispered.

"A lady who may speak her mind, dress to please herself, and befriend anyone she wishes to. But most of all, love the gentleman who has held her heart for longer than she can remember. Do you suppose the gentleman would approve of my wishes?" A hopeful expression lit her face.

"I have faith he approves wholeheartedly because you have held his heart for longer than he ever realized. Even when he thought he would never have a chance with you because of the circumstances out of his control. Do you suppose the lady would approve of my wishes?"

Abigail smiled. "And what might those wishes be?"

Lucas bent to whisper in her ear. "A lifetime of loving him every day. Passionate nights spent in his bed. And children for his father to spoil."

Abigail nodded, with tears streaming down her cheeks. "Yes, she will approve."

"Excellent," Lucas murmured. Before he could kiss Abigail, someone pounded on the door. "Go away," he yelled.

The pounding continued. "Lord Gray, we must leave. It has grown past the hour for your return. I am sorry I fell asleep."

"Damn," Lucas muttered. He peered out the window and saw the gray sky fading away into the soft light of the day. He rose to his feet, helping Abigail to rise. "Ready the carriage. We shall be ready soon." Lucas brushed his lips across Abigail's. "I am sorry, love. We must hurry."

He rushed to dress and helped Abigail back into her nightgown, wrapping her coat tightly around her. "The next time you wear this, it will be in our bedchamber and upon our bed."

Abigail lifted one shoulder. "Perhaps I might tempt you elsewhere with it."

She winked as she sauntered toward the door, her hips swaying in a seductive swing. She already tempted him and they hadn't even parted yet.

Lucas caught her and pulled her back against him. "As long as no one else catches a sight of your wanton display, then you may tempt me anywhere or anytime."

He tilted her head back and ravished her lips one last time before they departed. He groaned as he pulled away. His body ached for Abigail again. He hurried them to the carriage and ordered the coachman to make the return with haste.

Abigail snuggled into his arms and they held hands and whispered soft words of affection during the ride. Once they arrived back at his aunt and uncle's home, he noticed Duncan striding back and forth, looking at his pocket watch. His cousin wrenched the door open and whistled. Duncan grabbed Abigail from the carriage and soon Selina appeared at the door with a blanket. She rushed outside to wrap it around Abigail. Then, Duncan threw Abigail over his shoulder, muttering about an inconsiderate Englishman who seduced innocent misses.

Abigail's giggles floated back to him. She held her head up and blew Lucas a kiss. Lucas stood on the stoop of the carriage and grabbed at the imaginary kiss within his reach, then pressed it against his heart.

The kiss of a new beginning.

Chapter Twenty-Six

"I apologize. I have promised away all my dances," Abigail repeated to another gentleman who was requesting her hand for a dance.

When, in fact, she had promised away none of them. She held them all for one gentleman who had yet to appear. She hadn't seen Lucas since he stole her away for an evening of passion. Nor had he sent his excuses or any more flowers. If Abigail didn't hold faith in their love, she would believe he had only meant to share a tryst with her. However, she refused to acknowledge Lucas as a scoundrel who meant to keep their relationship private. There had to be a perfect explanation for what kept him away. Only, she held no clue what it might be.

However, it might also explain how everyone had treated her of late. When she came down to breakfast the morning after she spent with Lucas, Aunt Susanna had fussed over her and Selina had acted like she held another secret she couldn't reveal. Then, throughout the day, all her friends had arrived and regarded her with secret smiles and stars in their eyes. The same behavior had repeated itself each day since then. One of them always wanted to whisk her away from the Forresters' townhome.

Just the evening before, Colebourne had arrived for dinner and appeared quite pleased with himself. When Abigail questioned him about his behavior, he had changed the subject, suggesting a game of chess after dinner. Abigail had agreed and spent the game asking about Lucas, without drawing too much interest in his whereabouts. But the duke had only mumbled about how Lucas prepared for a trip he would embark on soon. Which only confused Abigail because Lucas had never mentioned leaving London.

Still, she kept a firm hold on her belief in Lucas.

"Who have you promised them to?" Evelyn asked.

Charlie watched the new set begin and there wasn't any gentleman walking toward them to escort Abigail onto the ballroom floor. "Which gentleman is not claiming your hand? I will set Sinclair on him."

Abigail rolled her eyes. "I do not need Sinclair to defend my honor."

"Why ever not? A gentleman has wronged you. Sinclair will make it right," Charlie explained.

"There is no need," Abigail insisted.

Charlie narrowed her gaze when Abigail turned her head to the side, refusing to meet Charlie's eyes. "Because you lied. Abigail Cason, Miss Honesty, has told fibs all evening. Perhaps even longer than we may think."

"Hush," Abigail hissed.

"She is holding out for Lucas," Gemma interrupted.

"Gemma," Abigail warned.

"I think it is sweet. She has promised all her dances to Lucas, and he is clueless," Gemma continued.

"Ahh." Jacqueline sighed.

"Oh. It is so romantic," Selina gushed.

Abigail looked around the ballroom, standing on her tiptoes to look over the dancers. "Or foolish. He has not even shown, nor do I expect he will."

Abigail turned back to her friends. They were glancing at each other with sappy expressions. When they noticed her attention on them, they looked away, taking an interest in the other dancers.

"What are you not sharing with me?" Abigail asked.

Her friends' expressions swiftly changed to panic. Abigail glanced around, but nothing appeared out of the ordinary. Each of her friends' husbands shared a drink in the corner. They surrounded someone, but Abigail didn't care who had snared their attention. She found the Forresters standing next to Colebourne and another gentleman Abigail had never met. Everything seemed normal. However, it didn't explain her friends' strange behavior.

"Well?" Abigail asked again, focusing her attention on Gemma.

Gemma was a sentimental mess with her pregnancy. Her behavior constantly changed between being sappy and weepy. She knew her friend couldn't resist sharing the secret they all held.

Gemma's eyes widened, darting back and forth between Charlie and Selina. A confession slipped forth. "Selina is expecting."

Abigail hugged Selina. "You are? How far along are you? I bet Susanna and Ramsay can hardly contain their excitement."

"Ahh . . . That is . . . I . . ." Selina stuttered out an explanation.

"I never even thought to ask about Duncan's reaction. He must be over the moon," Abigail added.

Before Selina responded to Abigail's questions, the dance set ended, and the servants carried in chairs and set them in rows. Once they filled the entire dance floor except for a small area near the front, the musicians started playing a waltz.

Abigail looked at Selina for an explanation, but Selina mouthed, "I am expecting?" to Gemma. Gemma winced and shrugged.

Abigail frowned. "You are not with child?"

"Ahh . . ."

A finger tapped on Abigail's shoulder, drawing her attention away from Selina's explanation. She turned to find Lucas holding out a rose to her.

"I would like to request your hand for the waltz playing. Although, there are rumors floating around how you have promised all your dances for this evening."

She took the rose and held it to her face to hide her smile of satisfaction at his arrival. "Only for you."

Abigail lowered the rose, and Lucas breathed a sigh of relief at her enchanting smile. He held out his hand. "Shall we?"

Abigail nodded, handing the rose to Selina. Lucas escorted them to the small area and swept her into his arms. They glided around smoothly, and Abigail relied on Lucas to guide them. She couldn't remember the steps because he wrapped her up in his spell. While in his arms, she floated in happiness. With each dip and turn, she clung to Lucas, and her eyes locked with his. She forgot the other guests as the melody bonded them together into one.

Abigail had never shared a dance with Lucas in a crowded ballroom for his peers to watch. His act declared his intentions toward her, causing Abigail to fall in love with him all over again. When the dance ended, he bowed to her and Abigail dipped into a curtsy. Then, to her surprise, he dropped to one knee. A hush fell over the ballroom floor at his display.

"Lucas?"

"Abigail, I love you with all my heart and I wish to express my love for you to the world. Not so long ago, I was a fool who refused to appreciate the rare gem you are. After a few harsh words from those I love and many miserable days, I saw how my life was without you. A dull existence of loneliness. You alone are what brightens my days. We have already spoken of your forgiveness and now I am asking you to make each of my days full of your sunshine. Abigail, will you do me the honor of becoming my wife?"

Tears streamed down Abigail's cheeks at Lucas's bold statement. His declaration spoke more than only asking her to become his wife. His proposal spoke of his decision to disregard the structures of society and spend a lifetime with her at his side. Abigail raised her gaze when each member of his family formed a line behind him, declaring their support.

She covered her mouth with a sob. Their act left her speechless. While they always offered words of encouragement and support, this act alone showed everyone what she meant to them. It showed Abigail their love.

Abigail started nodding.

"Yes?" Lucas asked, unsure of her reaction.

Lucas avoided Abigail for the past week, because he didn't want to ruin his surprise. If he even spent one moment in her company, he would have whisked her away to Scotland. However, he resisted because she deserved to understand how much she meant to him. He anxiously waited for her answer. Once her tears fell, he feared she would refuse him. But she put his fears to rest with the simple answer of yes.

"Yes! Yes!" Abigail sobbed, dropping to her knees next to Lucas.

"Yes!" Lucas shouted. He drew Abigail in his arms and gave her a kiss no one would ever forget.

He deepened the kiss, savoring her answer a while longer. Abigail clung to him and returned his kiss with a passion that would cause many of the ladies present to blush.

A hand slapped him on the back. "As much as it warms my heart, Abigail has answered yes. Perhaps you should wed before you cause much more of a scandal," Colebourne suggested.

Lucas reluctantly pulled away. His father was correct. He helped Abigail to her feet and enjoyed the blush highlighting her features. A becoming color he would find pleasure gazing upon in the years to come.

"Shall we?" Lucas pointed to the altar now in front of the rows of chairs.

"Now?" Abigail squeaked.

"I do not know of any better time. Do you?" Lucas squeezed her hands.

Abigail shook her head, her smile widening. She glanced around and noticed the guests filling into the chairs, with their family in the first two rows. Her tears started again when she noticed the two rows behind them were the servants from town and Colebourne Manor.

"May I have the honor of escorting you down the aisle?" Colebourne held out his arm.

"It would be my honor," Abigail whispered.

Lucas took his place at the front. Her friends enclosed her in hugs, and Selina pressed the rose back into her hand. Aunt Susanna wiped away her tears before Ramsay escorted her to their chairs. Once everyone took their seats, the musicians started a lifting melody as Colebourne walked her toward Lucas.

Before handing her off, he pressed his hands around hers. "You have made me a very happy old man this evening."

Abigail pressed a kiss to his cheek. "Thank you for your love, Poppa."

Colebourne beamed at her affectionate name and handed her to Lucas.

Lucas clutched her hands. "I love you, Abigail Cason."

"I love you, Lucas Gray," Abigail whispered.

There wasn't a dry eye amongst the ladies during the ceremony. Lucas's romantic gesture sent a buzz through the ton. Each mama professed they would expect nothing less for their daughters. Each unmarried lady made a wish for a Lucas Gray of their own. Each married lady hoped their husbands took note. And each gentleman cursed Lucas Gray for making their efforts inadequate compared to his. Now, they must step up their attempts to keep the ladies in their lives happy.

Once the ceremony ended, Colebourne made a toast, and the guests danced to a few more waltzes. Many hours later, the bride and groom were nowhere to be seen. However, the celebration continued into the early morning hours with tales of how the couple fell in love, each one different and more elaborate than the last.

But then, only a few knew the true story of Lucas and Abigail's love. It involved a matchmaking father, an aunt and uncle who acted as co-conspirators, and interfering cousins and their spouses.

And each one of them used a bit of madness to make the match complete.

Epilogue

Abigail rolled over to find her husband shaking his head with a smile on his face. "Good morning, Lord Gray."

Abigail's husky whisper washed over Lucas. "Good morning, Lady Gray. I had hoped I had worn you out enough for a sound rest. However, your restless slumber spoke otherwise."

Abigail held a wicked smile as she caressed her hand along his chest. "Perhaps I need to expound more energy before I fall asleep. Do you know how I might do that?"

Lucas groaned when her hand wrapped around his cock. "I might have a few suggestions I can show you."

Abigail pouted. "Only a few?"

Lucas rolled her over and pressed into her palm. "Oh, more than a few, my wanton wife. If you wish, we may begin my suggestions now."

Lucas wrapped his hand around hers and guided her hand up and down his cock. Abigail's eyes drifted shut as she felt the power beneath their grip. She knew her husband had much to teach her, and she was more than eager to learn.

"Shall we?" Lucas whispered in her ear.

"Yes." A breathy moan escaped her lips.

Over the next few hours, Lucas showed Abigail a few of his suggestions. Each of them started with a whispered scandalous description before he showed them to her. When Abigail fell asleep in her husband's arms, she never moved once. She lay content, nestled in his love. When they awoke, they were ready to experience a lifetime of love by each other's side.

~~~~~~

Lucas and Abigail walked into the drawing room after they enjoyed a private dinner in Lucas's suite. They had learned the entire family had gathered for dinner, and they wanted to express their gratitude before they left for their honeymoon on the morrow. Their family met them with a round of applause and hugs. Everyone offered their congratulations, taking credit for their union. Which caused a debate to erupt about who had made the match.

"To my most successful match to date," Colebourne boasted, lifting his glass in a toast.

"Your match? No. The match occurred under my roof," Ramsay argued.

"Your Scottish hide is not taking credit for my son's marriage."

"Well, I am. Because once again ye English didn't plan yer battle well," Ramsay baited him.

"At least we English know how to battle. The Scottish resort to stealing to win," Colebourne taunted.

Ramsay stood. "Is ye remark toward my son for stealing Selina?"

Colebourne shrugged. "If that is how you wish to take it, who am I to argue."

"If Duncan didn't steal Selina, then Abigail would never have become my wife," Lucas tried to intervene with simple logic.

Colebourne and Ramsay stared at Lucas with exasperation, then started laughing. Aunt Susanna joined in, their merriment confusing everyone else.

Ramsay wiped the tears from his eyes. "Can ye believe your boy?"

"I tried, but obviously I failed." Colebourne chortled.

"Excuse me. I am standing right here," Lucas muttered.

Abigail squeezed his hand in support. But she couldn't hide back her laughter any longer and joined in. Soon, the entire room laughed along. Try as he might, he didn't understand the humor of the situation. But it would appear the joke was on him.

Aunt Susanna was the one who took pity on him. "Your father never would have allowed your marriage to Selina to go through. If Duncan and Selina never admitted to their feelings, we had another plan in place."

Lucas narrowed his gaze at his father. "What plan?"

Colebourne smirked. "One must never reveal a plan in case they may need to use it at a future date."

Lucas nodded in complete understanding of what his father might have sacrificed to make Lucas admit to his love for Abigail. He drew Abigail's hand to his lips and placed a soft kiss across her knuckles. "I agree."

Who was Lucas to argue with a man who created mischief just to secure his loved ones' happiness? It was the same happiness his father had enjoyed for a brief spell before he suffered a tragic loss so profound he never thought his father would recover from. But when five girls who suffered a similar loss arrived, they had formed a family who helped each other through the heartache to survive stronger than ever.

A family he would help grow with Abigail.

He turned to look at her, enjoying the antics of his father and uncle. The day she walked into his life was the day his own heartache began to mend. The day he met his soul mate. There was nobody he loved more than Abigail. She was kindness, beauty, grace, forgiveness, all packaged into one amazing woman he was proud to call his wife. He couldn't wait for the day when their little ones played on the floor at their feet.

Lucas was madly in love with Abigail.

Abigail sensed Lucas's gaze on her and turned to stare at the wonderment in his eyes. Their family joked around them and Abigail soaked up the warmth. She now understood what family meant. Not always were they members related by blood, but also by friendship. Friendship that helped you through the heartache of losing a loved one. Friendship that welcomed you with open arms, laughing and crying with you through your trials and tribulations. Friends that offered you a special blend of love in the only way a family could.

Yesterday, she had pledged a lifetime to Lucas, a gentleman she held a love for so profoundly she could never explain. She might have hero-worshipped him as a young girl. But as she grew older, the love for him had only expanded in her heart. Now, she stood next to her best friend, her lover, her husband, a man who would make every day of their marriage a dream come true. Soon their children would join in the laughter and playfulness.

Abigail long ago fell head over heels in love with Lucas.

And with each year of their love, they would find a new sense of joy.

~~~~~

After his guests left and Lucas and Abigail retired to their room, Colebourne toasted his late wife's painting.

"We did it, Olivia. The boy has found his happiness. I apologize that I never listened to you all those years ago after you met Abigail. Forcing Lucas into the betrothal with Selina was a colossal mistake. However, Selina found her happiness with Duncan. Abigail and Lucas are perfect for each other. And the other girls married their soul mates. It took me a few years, but I now understand how Abigail charmed you. Because she has charmed me the same."

He took a drink of his finest whiskey. "There are even babies soon to come. I wish you were here because I miss you greatly. I love you, my sweet Olivia."

One always wondered why Colebourne went to the extreme with his matchmaking since it always turned into a madness that was out of his control. But one only had to see that love and madness traveled hand in hand. It was his greatest wish to leave his family with the legacy of his matchmaking madness.

Because the madness of love always prevailed.

~~~

Dear Lovely Readers,

I hope you have enjoyed reading all the books in the Matchmaking Madness series. I have thoroughly loved writing about Uncle Theo's mischief in finding soul mates for his wards and son. Each character and their journey to finding love holds a special place in my heart. It saddens me to bring the series to an end. However, the characters will make appearances in my next series. I'm busy writing a series revolved around the Worthington siblings I introduced throughout the Matchmaking Madness series. Stay in touch with my newsletter where I will share the progress of the books.

Thank you for all your kind words & support.

Happy Reading,

Laura

~~~

If you would like to hear my latest news then visit my website www.lauraabarnes.com to join my mailing list.

~~~

"Thank you for reading How the Lord Married His Lady. Gaining exposure as an independent author relies mostly on word-of-mouth, so if you have the time and inclination, please consider leaving a short review wherever you can."

Author Laura A. Barnes

International selling author Laura A. Barnes fell in love with writing in the second grade. After her first creative writing assignment, she knew what she wanted to become. Many years went by with Laura filling her head full of story ideas and some funny fish songs she wrote while fishing with her family. Thirty-seven years later, she made her dreams a reality. With her debut novel *Rescued By the Captain*, she has set out on the path she always dreamed about.

When not writing, Laura can be found devouring her favorite romance books. Laura is married to her own Prince Charming (who for some reason or another thinks the heroes in her books are about him) and they have three wonderful children and two sweet grandbabies. Besides her love of reading and writing, Laura loves to travel. With her passport stamped in England, Scotland, and Ireland; she hopes to add more countries to her list soon.

While Laura isn't very good on the social media front, she loves to hear from her readers. You can find her on the following platforms:

You can visit her at ***www.lauraabarnes.com*** to join her mailing list.

Website: http://www.lauraabarnes.com

Amazon: https://amazon.com/author/lauraabarnes

Goodreads: https://www.goodreads.com/author/show/16332844.Laura_A_Barnes

Facebook: https://www.facebook.com/AuthorLauraA.Barnes/

Instagram: https://www.instagram.com/labarnesauthor/

Twitter: https://twitter.com/labarnesauthor

TikTok: https://www.tiktok.com/@labarnesauthor

BookBub: https://www.bookbub.com/profile/laura-a-barnes

Desire more books to read by Laura A. Barnes

Enjoy these other historical romances:

~~~

Matchmaking Madness Series:

How the Lady Charmed the Marquess

How the Earl Fell for His Countess

How the Rake Tempted the Lady

How the Scot Stole the Bride

How the Lady Seduced the Viscount

How the Lord Married His Lady

~~~

Tricking the Scoundrels Series:

Whom Shall I Kiss... An Earl, A Marquess, or A Duke?

Whom Shall I Marry... An Earl or A Duke?

I Shall Love the Earl

The Scoundrel's Wager

The Forgiven Scoundrel

~~~

Romancing the Spies Series:

Rescued By the Captain

Rescued By the Spy

Rescued By the Scot

Printed in Great Britain
by Amazon

79810135R00139